WILLIE HORTON

WILLIE HORTON

Detroit's Own
Willie the Wonder

GRANT ELDRIDGE AND KAREN ELIZABETH BUSH

WAYNE STATE UNIVERSITY PRESS DETROIT

Great Lakes Books
Detroit Biography Series for Young Readers

First Lady of Detroit: The Story of Marie-Thérèse Guyon,
Mme Cadillac, by Karen Elizabeth Bush, 2001

The Reuther Brothers—Walter, Roy, and Victor,
by Mike Smith and Pam Smith, 2001

Albert Kahn: Builder of Detroit, by Roger Matuz, 2001

Willie Horton: Detroit's Own Willie the Wonder
by Grant Eldridge and Karen Elizabeth Bush, 2001

Library of Congress Cataloging-in-Publication Data

Eldridge, Grant.
    Willie Horton, Detroit's own Willie the Wonder / Grant Eldridge
and Karen Elizabeth Bush.
        p. cm. — (Detroit biography series for young readers)
    ISBN 0-8143-3013-4 (alk. paper) — ISBN 0-8143-3025-8 (pbk. :
alk. paper)
    1. Horton, Willie, 1942—Juvenile literature. 2. Baseball players—
United states—Biography—Juvenile literature. [1. Horton, Willie, 1942-
2. Baseball players. 3. African Americans—Biography.] I. Bush, Karen
Elizabeth. II. Title. III. Series.
    GV865.H63 F53 2001
    796.357'092—dc21

                                                    2001004772

CONTENTS

♪♪♪ **1** ♪♪♪

World Champions

THE LOU BROCK PLAY

O ne of the important facts of life is that, in baseball, even if the teams are forced to play them all, there still are only seven games in a World Series. Once a single team has won four of those games, the series is over.

Sometimes a team wins a World Series in four straight games. Sometimes it takes five or six games. Some years it takes all seven games before it's all over and decided. No matter how long a series lasts, once your team has lost three games, you know that losing just one more game means that you're whipped. All you can do then is go home.

On October 7, 1968, Detroit baseball fans knew all too well that, since their team had lost a game, won a game, and then lost two more, they had three games in the "lost" column. It also meant that the Detroit Tigers were down three to one. By 1968, baseball teams had been playing World Series games for eighty-one years. In all that time, only two teams had ever come back from being down three to one.

The Detroit Tigers needed to win three straight ball games if they were going to win the World Series. That was a pretty tough assignment. To make matters worse, it was already the fifth inning of game five, the Tigers were trailing the St. Louis Cardinals by a score of three to two, and the Cardinals had their best runner on second base, in "scoring position." Any sort of base hit would make the score four to two in the Cardinals' favor.

The Tigers had won 103 games during the 1968 season, and in almost half of those they had come from behind to win. In fact, in thirty games they'd won a ball game the very last time a Tiger came up to bat. The Tigers knew they could win when the odds were against them, but on the afternoon of October 7th, to the fans in the stands it didn't look as if the home team had much of a chance.

Over the previous two days at Tiger Stadium, the Tigers had dropped two straight games in front of the home crowd. The first loss—in the first World Series game to be played in the old ball park in twenty-three years—was bad enough. The second loss was worse. The mighty St. Louis Cardinals had whipped the Tigers' pitching great Denny McLain by a score of no fewer than ten runs to one.

Cardinal Lou Brock had to be thinking about those ten runs now. He danced along the baseline, taunting Mickey Lolich, the Tiger pitcher. Off the field, Brock was as nice a man as you'd care to meet. But when it came to running the bases, he could be pretty cocky. He knew just how good he was, and he wasn't about to let anybody forget it—especially not the opposing pitcher. If it had been a playground game, Brock probably would have been chanting "nyah, nyah, nyah—can't stop me! Can't stop the Cardinals!"

So far in the series, the fleet Cardinal outfielder had stolen at least one base in every game. He had seven stolen bases in all. In Game Two, he'd stolen two bases. In Game Three, he stole three. Now he edged off second, ready to fly all the way home on anything that even looked like a base hit.

Julian Javier was at bat. Lolich fired the ball toward the plate. Javier swung and sent a line drive into left field. The hit was "in front of the runner," making the play a little easier to make, but it still was a solid base hit—all that Brock needed—and he dashed toward home plate.

Now, if he was thinking anything at all, it probably was that Tiger catcher Bill Freehan had only thrown him out one time in the series. Maybe he also was remembering that the Tiger left fielder, Willie Horton, wasn't supposed to be in top form defensively. (In fact, before the 1968 series was over, Willie would be taken out of the game in the late innings a total of four times to make room for a different player. This was in part because Willie's knees were bothering him. Once he finished his last turn at bat in a game, manager Mayo Smith often sat him down. When the score was close, Mayo wanted men in the field who—at least "according to the book"—could run faster than Willie did.)

But this was only the fifth inning. Willie's bat might be

needed before the game was over, so he was still playing left field when Javier's ball headed in that direction. The 53,634 fans in the ball park held their breaths. All over Detroit and Michigan, people were doing the same thing. Men and women in offices and restaurants, children and teachers in schools, shoppers in stores, and even people on street corners holding transistor radios, took deep breaths and crossed their fingers.

Back at Tiger Stadium, out there in left field, Willie knew exactly what had to be done, and he knew that he was the man to do it.

Ballplayers talk about "reaching back and getting something extra" when they're in a tough spot. Willie charged forward and fielded Javier's ball cleanly on one hop, and then, without breaking stride, he reached back and threw the ball as hard as he could. All the force of his running and all the strength of his arm went into that throw. The ball came into the infield on the fly, past Don Wert, the "cutoff man." It bounced once and smacked hard into the waiting glove of catcher Bill Freehan just about chest high. Freehan spun with the catch and blocked the plate.

Brock didn't slide. All season long he hadn't bothered to slide into home plate—scorning opposing team attempts to throw him out. One more time, Brock came home standing up straight. At the very last moment, he tried to reach the plate with his left foot. But he didn't slide, and he couldn't reach past Bill Freehan. The Tiger catcher stood there as solid as a wall, ball in hand, waiting to tag the runner.

The tag came down. "Yer OUT!" cried umpire Doug Harvey.

It all happened in a heartbeat. The Cardinals poured out of their dugout, screaming. They shouted. They argued. It made no difference. Brock was out. There was still one more out in the inning, but anything after that spectacular play at the plate meant little. The Cardinal rally was over. The Cards were still ahead, but only by one run. They didn't score again in that ball game.

The Tigers went on to win game five by a score of five to three. Then they traveled to St. Louis, where they won games six and seven. In all the rest of the World Series, the Cardinals managed to score just two more runs against the Tigers, and when they came back home to Detroit at the end of the week, the 1968 Detroit Tigers were the World Champions of major league baseball.

If it were possible for anybody to be happier than the people of Detroit, it would have to have been the Tigers themselves. From the moment Bill Freehan caught Tim McCarver's pop-up to end the seventh game of the series, the Tiger clubhouse in St.

THE PLAY AT THE PLATE. This famous photo from the 1968 World Series shows Bill Freehan taking Willie Horton's throw and blocking Cardinal runner Lou Brock, whose left foot almost—but not quite—reaches home plate. (Tony Spina photo, courtesy of the Walter P. Reuther Library, Wayne State University.)

Louis and the streets in Detroit were one big celebration. In St. Louis, the Tigers poured champagne on each other, somersaulted into the whirlpool bath (used normally for soaking aching muscles), hugged, and laughed, and cried.

"Man, oh, man!" Willie Horton kept saying. "I looked over the top of the left field roof in the seventh inning, and there was Rudolph the Rednosed Reindeer. Christmas came early! Man, oh, man! I've never been this happy in my life. Never! Never! Never! Man, oh, man! . . . It's just like being a kid on Christmas!"

Julio Moreno, who pitched batting practice for the team that year, took off his uniform and put on his good suit, ready to catch the plane back to Detroit. This was a serious mistake. Mickey Stanley and Dick McAuliffe promptly picked him up and tossed him into the whirlpool. Willie grinned at Moreno and started singing "Jingle Bells."

So many people crowded the airport in Detroit to celebrate the Tigers' arrival that, once the plane landed, the airport had to be shut down. The bus carrying the team from the plane headed back to Tiger Stadium so the players could pick up their cars and start to work their way home. It was late in the evening, but the city streets still were so full of people celebrating that the bus had to crawl along. All over the city and suburbs, the following morning's papers carried the headline, "WE WIN!!!" Many would be delivered with handwritten messages from newspaper carriers scrawled above the headline. "Good Morning, Tiger Fans!" a Brighton, Michigan newspaper boy wrote over and over, until he'd shared his joy at the Tigers' victory with every person on his route.

Willie Horton's throw from left field to cut off Lou Brock at home plate had been the turning point in the World Series. "It lifted us," Bill Freehan told the newspaper reporters.

All that winter, people talked about the Lou Brock play. Willie heard them talking, and he worked hard to make people understand that it wasn't just his throw that made the difference. "It wasn't just one man's effort," he kept saying. Scouting reports showed that Brock usually didn't slide, he explained. Brock was so fast, outfielders had given up trying to throw him out. Knowing that, Brock had gotten careless. With a good throw, there always was a chance to get him. Besides, it was up to catcher Bill Freehan to make the play. It was Bill who had to decide whether the cutoff man, Don Wert, should catch the ball, or if it should come all the way to the plate. Years later, when *The Detroit Tigers: A Movie* was made, Willie was still protesting. "[The play on

11

Brock?] We all did things as a *team*," he said. "I made the throw, but it was the *combination* of Freehan, Don Wert, and Willie Horton and the support of Mickey Stanley [at shortstop]" that made the difference.

The Summer of 1967

Twenty, thirty, creeping up to forty years have passed, and people still talk about Lou Brock and Willie Horton and Bill Freehan. It was an exciting play, all right—part of what baseball is all about. But the thing that made it such an important play was something much bigger than anything that could be found on a baseball diamond.

Just one year before the 1968 World Series, Detroit, Michigan, had been a divided town. In 1967, the tension was so high between black Detroiters and white Detroiters that, in July of that year, a major riot broke out. Before it was over, the riot turned block after block of the city into nothing more than piles of rubble and ashes. Homes and businesses were burned, windows were smashed, and stores were looted. It was almost as if war had been declared. Certainly there were enough soldiers! For weeks and weeks, tanks and armored vehicles rumbled through Detroit streets as the U.S. National Guard patrolled the neighborhoods. Just as in a war, families were left homeless. And, as they are in war, people were killed. Forty-three Detroiters lost their lives during those terrible days. The Detroit riot of 1967 was the worst civil disturbance (to date) in all U.S. history.

When the riot began it was a Sunday afternoon, and there was a ball game down at the corner of Michigan and Trumbull. From inside Tiger Stadium, fans could hear sirens and see (and even smell) smoke. Rumors floated around, but no one knew for sure what was happening. It wasn't until the game was over and fans began to leave that people heard how many fires there were—and how many men and women were in the streets rioting. By that time, roads were blocked and whole sections of the city were shut down. Willie Horton, one year away from making that famous throw to home plate, didn't take time to change clothes after the game. He just hurried toward home. "I'll never forget riding to the Livernois area, the 12th Street area," he said later. "I'm in my uniform and seeing these . . . seeing this happen. It was a shock. . . . [I thought] this is Detroit; this is not happen-

THE NATIONAL GUARD ARRIVES. The 1967 Detroit riot began in the streets directly behind Tiger Stadium. In this photograph, National Guard troopers spill off a truck, hurrying to stop the looting and burning that is visible in the distance. (Tony Spina photo, courtesy of the Walter P. Reuther Library, Wayne State University.)

ing. And that's when I realized what was going on. . . . People were shooting, people scurrying. . . . What can I do? What can I say? And I [found] myself walking down . . . seeing buildings on 12th Street . . . people breaking in, and I'm trying to talk to people."

It would take far more than Willie Horton's efforts to stop the riots that tore Detroit apart that summer. Yet with the coming of fall, an uneasy peace settled over the town. Baseball went on down at the Corner. In fact, the Tigers almost won the pennant that year. But on the very last day of the season, with one out in the bottom of the ninth inning, Dick McAuliffe hit into a double play. He hadn't hit into a double play all that year. Now, with one swing

SNIPERS. This picture of a National Guardsman scanning surrounding buildings in search of snipers became the definitive portrait of the Detroit riots. (Tony Spina photo, courtesy of the Walter P. Reuther Library, Wayne State University.)

of the bat, the Tigers lost both the ball game and the American League Championship. It was an awful moment for the whole team. Afterward, Willie's teammate Gates Brown told a reporter than he'd never seen so many grown men cry.

The winter of 1967–1968 came and went in a city desperately in need of some kind of healing. Its people needed a direction—something, anything that they could do to make things better. The Tigers, at home with their families until February, worried about the city. But they also spent a lot of that winter thinking and talking about what they needed to do to make up for that last, heartbreaking ball game. Next year, by golly—next year. . . . To a man, the Tigers were absolutely determined that they were going to win everything—the American League Championship, the World Series, *everything*—in 1968.

Down at the corner of Michigan and Trumbull, the old ballpark quietly awaited the return of spring, baseball, and Willie Horton—baseball's "designated healer."*

---

* This term was coined by newspaper columnist George Cantor, and it first appeared in his book, *The Tigers of '68* (Dallas: Taylor Publishing, 1997).

⚾⚾⚾ **2** ⚾⚾⚾

Virginia Mornings

JUST BEING A KID

It's hard to get much deeper into the Appalachian mountains than the little town of Arno, Virginia. Arno is a mining camp—not really a town at all. It's so small, it doesn't even show up on a map. Modern travel brochures about Wise County, where Arno is located, don't mention industry, schools, shopping centers, or fancy resorts. There aren't any. Instead, they describe clear, cold trout streams and talk about woods so quiet that the silence is broken only by the sound of birds singing.

Wise County wasn't much different when Willie Horton was born. Back in the 1940s, there weren't any tourists reading travel brochures. The only business in Arno was mining coal. Coal built the town and gave employment to most of the people who lived there. Clinton Horton, Willie's father, was no exception. He worked long, hard hours in the coal mines, trying to earn enough money to support his family. He worked as much as the bosses would let him. He had to feed one of the largest families in Wise County.

Clinton Horton and his wife Lillian had twenty-one children—eight boys and thirteen girls. With money for medicine and doctors in short supply, seven of the young Hortons didn't live long enough to grow up. But that still left Clinton and Lillian with fourteen children to raise. The last one of those fourteen, William Wattison Horton, was born on October 18, 1942. The county clerk registered the baby's name as "William Watterson Horton," but no matter. Clinton and Lillian knew the difference.

Although by the time Willie was born many of his older brothers and sisters were grown up and out on their own, there

15

ARNO, VIRGINIA, AND DERBY/ARNO. In uptown Arno, "company houses" (built by the mining companies for miners and their families) and an old garage are tucked under the hill on one side of the street. A mountain stream runs along the other side. There wasn't much more to Arno back when Willie was born there—just a few more houses, the company store, and, of course, the working mine itself. (Tim C. Cox Photo/Graphics, Norton, Virginia.)

still was a houseful of people calling Lillian and Clinton "Mom" and "Pop." Grandchildren, nieces, and nephews came to visit—and then came to stay. Every day when Willie came home from school, there were children all over the place. Just for good measure, there was always a dog or so somewhere, too. And then there was a white lady who was around a lot. She was just "there" from time to time—looking kind of different, but still part of everything that was happening. It would be years and years before Willie realized that the white lady was his own grandmother—Clinton Horton's mother.

With so many people eating, there were times—lots of times—when there wasn't enough food to go around. Willie knew what it was like to go to bed without supper because there wasn't any supper. He knew what it was like to be cold because, no matter how much coal his father dug out of the ground, there wasn't enough money to buy coal to heat the house. Eventually there was no work at all to be found in Arno. The mines shut down, and, looking for work, Pop moved the entire family to nearby Stonega—a real town, with 1,500 people in it. There, for a time at least, he could go back to digging coal.

But you didn't need money to have friends in Arno—or Stonega, either. You didn't need money to play outdoors, or to fish or explore the hills. Most of all you didn't need money to feel

Willie's Birthplace in Arno. All the houses on the road where Clinton and Lillian Horton lived have fallen down over the years. Willie took this picture of the place where they used to be. This is where, in the fall of 1942, Willie Horton was born. (Photo courtesy of Willie Horton.)

loved, and Willie was loved—by his parents, and by his brothers and sisters, and by all those nieces and nephews and cousins. And Willie loved them back.

One day Clinton looked at his son and asked, "What's the difference between a man living on the street and a rich man?"

That was easy. Willie answered right away. "The rich man is a success. He's got money!"

Clinton Horton shook his head. "But what's the difference apart from the money? What's the difference in God's eyes?"

Willie thought for a minute. There wasn't any difference. God didn't care about money. He didn't care about anything like that—not people's money, not their place in society, not even the color of their skin. All God cared about was that people were good and good to each other. After a little bit, Willie nodded to himself. He understood. His father wanted him to think about what was important in life. His father wanted him to realize that *character* was what mattered.

Willie was lucky. He grew up, as he said, "never seein' no difference" between black people and white people. But, in parts of the South in the late 1940s, sometimes it was hard to remember that God didn't care about the color of somebody's skin. Some white people treated African Americans as if they were not really "people" at all. Black families couldn't live in the same part of town as white families. Black children and white children went to different schools. Laws made it illegal for African Americans to use the same drinking fountains or toilets or public waiting rooms that white people did. And because the African American community didn't have much money, homes and schools and public facilities for black people were very, very poor when compared to the ones used by the rest of society.

Yet it wasn't as if everybody went around hating each other all the time. It was true that some whites despised African Americans for no reason other than their race. Those people went out of their way to hurt black families and humiliate them. The fact that they could get away with it was a constant reminder that there was something wrong with the way society worked. But for the most part, black people and white people were friendly. It was just that tradition and the law—and often the difference in how much money people had—kept them far enough apart that there really wasn't much they could do together.

Pop knew all about that. He'd lived with it all his life. That was why he saw to it that Willie kept on "not seein' no difference" but knew enough to judge a man by his character.

THE BEST BASEBALL DIAMOND

For eight-year-old Willie, this "segregation" business (keeping the races separate) was just the way things were. He didn't really take time to think about what it all meant. He was far too happy just being a kid. For that matter, in that part of Virginia not everything was segregated—at least not exactly. Sure, he and his friends lived in different parts of town, but except for when they went home at night, they were together just about all the time.

STONEGA, VIRGINIA. When the mines shut down in Arno, Clinton Horton moved his family to the larger town of Stonega. Its streets were a lot busier when Willie was a child, but much of the Stonega he knew is still there. The building on the left was the school. (Photo courtesy of Willie Horton.)

Segregation was something Willie didn't really learn about until he came north to live—or especially once he'd been to the Deep South. In Stonega, kids were just kids, and one of the things they did together was play baseball.

The Stonega field wasn't very good. It was bumpy and dusty and roughly marked out—not really the right shape. Six miles away from Stonega, in Appalachia—a town twice Stonega's size— there was a really good baseball field. The white children in Appalachia used it. Just about all the boys who played ball in Stonega wished they could play on that big field in Appalachia— Willie especially. He thought, and thought, and thought about it. It would be so wonderful to get to play on a field with real bases and a real home plate!

Over and over, Willie asked his father if he and his friends could go to Appalachia and play on the big diamond. Each time

19

THE RAILROAD TRACK. In Stonega, Willie lived in a house next to the railroad tracks. He was standing at just about the spot where this picture was taken, crying because his friends wouldn't go with him to Appalachia, when something made him start walking there by himself. He walked six miles down the track. It was a journey toward a career in baseball, and Willie tells people, "God came into my life that day." (Photo courtesy of Willie Horton.)

he asked, Pop said, "Yes." Pop didn't say much more than that; he just said "yes." So Willie kept asking. In the back of his mind, he was hoping that Pop would do something to make the other boys go with him to Appalachia. It was a long walk to get there—six miles down the railroad track—but it wasn't the walk that bothered him as much as having to go to a strange place and face all those strange boys alone. Still, the only answer he got was "yes" and nothing more, and one day Pop got a little mad.

"Look, Willie," Pop said. "Why do you keep asking me about it? I've told you that you can go see if you can play there. If you want that much to play, it's up to you to do something about it."

What Willie decided to do about it was try to talk his friends, James and Bunny, into coming along with him. But that didn't work, either.

"Willie, you're plain crazy!" The boys laughed at him. "We can't play on that fancy white boys' field! They'll mess us up good just for showing up there!"

Willie argued back. His parents had told him over and over again to look for the best in people. "It'll be okay," he said. "We'll just go and ask them. It won't hurt to ask."

His friends shook their heads in disbelief. Willie must think he lived in a perfect world, somewhere. In the Wise County they knew, no poor boy from a mining camp could be that sure of an easy welcome from an entire baseball team of white boys. James and Bunny went on home, sure that Willie was setting himself up for a whole lot of trouble.

Willie wasn't blind to the kind of problem he was facing. He knew why his friends were afraid. The boys didn't think about it much, but they'd all heard stories about people, especially black people, who were insulted or beaten up—or even worse—for trying to go places they weren't supposed to go. Willie was just plain scared to go to Appalachia alone, but he sure didn't dare go back and ask Pop about it again! He was frustrated and miserable and angry—and he was feeling thoroughly sorry for himself.

Under those circumstances, there was only one thing to do, and Willie did it. He started to cry. He stumbled along the dusty path, sobbing in earnest, not paying any attention to where he was going. He had walked past the church and was more or less headed toward the railroad tracks when he felt something take hold of him. It wasn't as though there was a hand on his shoulder or anything like that, but he felt himself turned hard—straight down toward those tracks. It seemed like the thing to do, so he walked in that direction. He stepped over the rail and stood on the ties, staring down the tracks toward Appalachia. He scrubbed at his eyes with the back of his hand and sniffed—loudly. He started to walk again, faster and faster—surer and surer. Maybe everything was going to be all right. Maybe baseball itself would make the difference. At least baseball was something that he and the strange white boys in Appalachia all knew about. It was something they shared. Suddenly not worried any more, Willie headed down the railroad tracks to Appalachia—all by himself.

There was another little town—just a few houses, really—between Stonega and Appalachia, and there, playing near the tracks, Willie saw a white boy. "Hey, there!" Willie called. "Want to come with me to Appalachia to play some baseball?"

"You're crazy," the boy replied, sounding a lot like Willie's

THE WOLVES. Willie Horton, suited up in a fancy new Little League uniform, stands with some of his fellow Wolves. The tall boy next to Willie is Larry Munsey, who walked most of the way with him from Stonega to Appalachia. (Photo courtesy of Willie Horton.)

friends had earlier that morning. "Those guys in Appalachia have uniforms and everything, and they play on that fancy field. They won't make room for guys like us." But the boy, whose name was Larry Munsey, didn't have anything better to do, so he fell into stride with Willie—still arguing as the two headed further down the tracks toward Appalachia.

It was a long walk, but it didn't seem that far to the boys. They took their time and wandered along, just talking. The spring sun was warm, and the air smelled good. They passed little streams and stopped to see if they could catch any suckers with their hands. They wandered into the woods to see how close they could come to squirrels. It was well into the afternoon before they arrived in Appalachia and wandered up to the playing field. It was

Posing Like the Big Leaguers Do. Willie and other Wolves squat down for this picture, trying to look like major league ballplayers lined up for a team portrait. Notice the "W" for Wolf on each uniform. (Photo courtesy of Willie Horton.)

just as if it had been arranged that way on purpose. They'd arrived exactly in time for Little League tryouts!

As it turned out, uniforms didn't matter at all. The coach of the team looked right past skin color, dust, and torn, dirty blue jeans. "Hi!" he said. "What positions do you boys play?"

Later on, that coach, Mr. Strong, would tell people that Willie tried out at every single position on the diamond and looked good in them all. Willie was hitting the ball so well, Strong asked a semiprofessional ballplayer to try throwing a couple of balls past him. Willie hit those pitches, too.

Munsey looked good in the tryouts, too, though not as good as Willie. Both he and Willie were asked to join the Appalachia Little League team. Nobody made much fuss about it, but adding

Willie to the team made the Wolves (they were sponsored by Wolf Furniture Store) one of the very first integrated Little League teams in that part of Virginia.

Things were even better than Willie hoped they would be. His parents were right. He had to trust in the goodness of people. Once he'd remembered that being good was the most important thing, he'd given things a chance to work out the right way. It took courage to put his belief in people to the test, but Willie had courage along with hope and faith. And, man, oh, man, had things ever worked out the right way! Now he understood more about how Mom and Pop felt about God. He would often tell people that God came into his life that day—it had to have been God who sent him on that first long walk down the railroad tracks to Appalachia. At the end of that walk, not only had Willie found friends he would keep until his dying day, he had taken his first steps in the direction he would follow for the rest of his life.

Many years later, long after his major league baseball career was over and long after he was established as a successful businessman, Willie was invited back to Virginia to be part of a radio show that was telling his life story. And lo and behold, there was Munsey! After all those years, the two men recognized each other instantly. They hugged and slapped each other on the back—and even got a little teary-eyed. And then they sat there talking about Coach Strong and all those white boys from Appalachia who let them play on their fancy baseball diamond.

⊙⊙⊙ **3** ⊙⊙⊙

The Motor City

In 1950, World War II was over and there wasn't as much demand for coal to fuel battleships and destroyers as there had been during wartime. Factories didn't have to build ships and tanks and airplanes, so they used less coal, too. Mine shafts went deeper and deeper as vein after vein of coal was dug up and hauled away. It was getting more and more expensive to reach the coal, and, once it was dug, now there were fewer and fewer places to sell it. Times were tough for mine owners. The mines in Stonega laid off some of their miners, and then they laid off still more of them. Eventually, the day came when the Stonega mines shut down altogether.

Clinton Horton needed to work to support his family, but there was no other work to be had in Stonega—or even in Appalachia. The few jobs there were went to other miners—usually white—who also found themselves looking for work when the mines closed down. Clinton and Lillian talked and talked about it. It looked as if the only way they could keep from starving was to leave Virginia and move to a city. There should be jobs aplenty in a big city.

But what city? Lillian Horton's aunt lived in Detroit, Michigan. As a matter of fact, Lillian visited her just a few years before, and Willie had gone along. Willie didn't remember much about the trip, but Lillian did. Now she reminded her husband that Detroit was a bustling, booming place. The auto industry was thriving; everybody was working. It was very different from Virginia. Besides, Detroit was in the North. Maybe there wouldn't be very much segregation there, and that might make it easier for Clinton to get a job.

At first, Clinton and Lillian went to Detroit alone. There were

DOWNTOWN DETROIT IN 1950. Detroit was a busy, bustling place in the middle of the twentieth century. Known as the "Motor City," it was prosperous first because of the automobile industry, and then because its auto plants were used for war-related manufacturing during World War II. (Courtesy of the Walter P. Reuther Library, Wayne State University.)

things that had to be settled before the whole family could move there, so Willie was sent to Kentucky to stay with his eldest sister. He missed everybody, but it was all right—sort of. And then, after a while, he went on to Kingsport, Tennessee. There he had a brother who would keep him until it was time for Willie to go home to Mom and Pop, wherever "home" was going to be. That was all right, too. Besides, in Kingsport, he could play baseball— real baseball, in a league—just as he had in Appalachia. Baseball made the days go by a lot faster. There would be a lot of those days; they needed to go by fast. It would be a whole year before it was time for the real move.

Five Hortons would live together in Detroit: Willie, his Mom and Pop (Clinton and Lillian), and two grandchildren who were just about Willie's age. At first, everybody's hopes were high. The family didn't have any money to speak of, but they did have a

THE RETAIL DISTRICT. During the '50s, Detroit shoppers crowded busy Woodward Avenue. The tall building on the right is the J. L. Hudson department store. Although this picture was taken in 1958, this is the way Detroit looked in 1950 when Willie's family first moved there. (Courtesy of the Walter P. Reuther Library, Wayne State University.)

place to live. Pop found a two-bedroom apartment on Avery and Canfield. That was good enough for right now. A year later, the family would move to West Forest Avenue. West Forest was on the north side of a group of apartment buildings called the "Jefferson Project," and one of Willie's sisters found her own apartment in the Jefferson Project.

The "projects" and nearby apartment buildings weren't like the nice apartments in other parts of Detroit. There wasn't even a kitchen or bathroom in the Horton apartment—not one of their own, at any rate. Mom Horton had to share cooking time with other people in the building, and if Willie wanted to go to the bathroom, he had to go outside the apartment and down the hall—hoping that the other tenants hadn't left too much of a mess in the community toilet. It wasn't very pleasant, but that was why the apartment was cheap enough for them to afford.

"Cheap" soon got to be even more important than it had been in Virginia. Living in Detroit was much more expensive than living in Stonega had been. There were no mountain streams with suckers swimming in them—bony, but good to eat. All food came from the supermarket. Rent had to be paid. School was expensive, too. Willie and the other children had to have clothes—not fancy, but clothes that fit and would keep them warm during Detroit winters. Worse, Willie's Pop couldn't find a job. No one was interested in hiring a former coal miner, and mining was all Clinton Horton had done for years and years. He took a series of part-time jobs, but nothing lasted very long—or paid very much. Mom did what she could to help. She took in ironing and collected bottles for the deposit money. Most of all, she watched all the time for ways to stretch a dollar—the way poor people learn to do.

Although Mom and Pop were struggling every day to pay bills and keep everyone fed, Willie didn't worry much about money. He was too busy! There were no ball games to play in—not right away, anyway. But the city of Detroit was building a freeway that ran straight down the middle of his neighborhood.

In the 1950s, most roads were just two lanes wide. Stopping for stop signs and traffic lights was just part of what people did as they drove from place to place. When Willie thought about a road that was four lanes wide, and that tunneled under cross streets so that people could drive straight through town without having to slow down—man, oh, man! He felt almost as if there were going to be rockets or airplanes flying along right next door. Of course, the John C. Lodge Freeway wasn't built yet, but seeing and listening to the heavy equipment the road builders were using was interesting, and sometimes it seemed as exciting as watching cars swoop by.

Day after day, Willie got up in the morning to watch as the huge bulldozers changed the face of Detroit. Other boys from the projects were there too, watching. In addition to seeing bulldozers push mountains of earth around, there were new friends to make. There were new things to talk about, too, as the boys hung over the barriers that kept them from getting too close to the men and equipment.

"Whatcha gonna be when you grow up, Willie?" his new friends asked. Willie really hadn't thought much about it. It might be fun and exciting to be a fireman, he thought. But what

THE JEFFRIES PROJECT. Willie's first home in Detroit was in the Jeffries Housing Project. Forest Avenue, the location of his parents' apartment, is at the upper right part of this picture. In the foreground you can see where the earth has been dug up to prepare the roadbed for the John C. Lodge Freeway. This picture was taken in 1952, just about the time ten-year-old Willie was hitting bottle caps across the freeway construction site. (Courtesy of the Walter P. Reuther Library, Wayne State University.)

Willie wanted most to be was a cowboy. He loved all the TV and movie cowboys. They were brave, and they rode wonderful horses, and they always beat the bad guys. Roy Rogers and Gene Autry were his favorites, but Willie loved them all: Roy and Gene, Hopalong Cassidy, the Lone Ranger, Wild Bill Elliot, Lash LaRue. The horses had wonderful names, too. Hoppy rode Topper, Gene Autry had Champion, and the Lone Ranger rode the great horse Silver. The Lone Ranger's sidekick Tonto sat bareback on a splashy spotted horse called Scout. Even Roy Rogers's wife, Dale Evans, had a horse with a name, although it was a funny one. She called her horse "Buttermilk." Willie's favorite horse, though, was Roy Rogers' beautiful palomino, Trigger. What a wonderful thing it would be if he could ride Trigger across the open range!

"Whatcha gonna be?" his friends asked again. Willie looked

back toward the construction site. "I dunno," he said. "A construction worker, maybe."

One thing Willie didn't think about was being a professional baseball player. Still, when his friends made up games to play, one of Willie's favorite games involved hitting bottle caps with a stick. The boys didn't run around bases or keep score. They just hit the bottle caps as far as they could—sometimes so far they couldn't hear them rattle when they landed on the street. Willie's bottle caps sailed farther than anybody else's. He felt strong as he picked up the next cap. Maybe he could make it go all the way across the freeway! His friends watched a little enviously. Not only did Willie's broomstick really make a loud "crack!" when it hit the bottle cap, Willie was really good at tossing each bottle cap in the air and hitting it at exactly the right moment before it hit the ground.

It's fun to be good at something, and Willie got more and more excited about just how good he was at this game. By dinnertime—and time to go home—he was fairly bursting with how good he was. He ran in the door shouting, "Mom! Mom! You shoulda seen me! I can hit bottle caps a mile! I can hit 'em lots farther than anybody else can!" He'd hardly paused for breath when he heard his father in the next room.

"Willie. . . ." Pop's voice had a warning note.

Willie knew what that meant. He wasn't supposed to brag. "I can really hit 'em, though," he muttered to himself.

It's good to have a Pop who keeps you in line and a Mom to hug you from time to time. That night, Willie's Mom was ready with a good hug. She and Pop were both proud of Willie, she said, even though he shouldn't have bragged so much about it. Maybe it wasn't a whole mile, but Mom believed he could hit those bottle caps hard. "You keep on practicing," she said. "It'll make you a better baseball player, too."

T-BALL IS FOR LITTLE KIDS

Baseball, for Willie, still was the best sport, but in Detroit it was hard to find a place to play. In the city, boys his age who wanted to play in any kind of organized ball—with sponsors to buy equipment and keep up the baseball diamonds—were supposed to play T-ball. Now, a guy who can hit a bottle cap a mile doesn't want to waste his time hitting a baseball off the top of a big wooden post like some little kid. Besides, Willie knew about real hitting. He had all that playing time in Virginia and Tennessee when he was hitting baseballs that were pitched right to him. Naw. T-ball was sissy stuff, and so Willie and his friends played softball, where they could have a real pitcher, instead of a dumb old tee.

Neighborhood people often hung around to watch the boys play. One day Willie and his friends realized that a strange man was following them around, watching their games day after day.

"Don't talk to strangers" was part of everything Willie had been taught. "Don't talk to strangers," and "don't ever hitchhike." He'd heard those things over and over. Once, in Virginia, he'd gone to the store for Mom. On the way back, a young man offered him a ride in a shiny car. "Oh, no!" Willie said. "No thank you. I'm takin' these things to my Mom, and my Pop would whip me if he knew I hitchhiked a ride." The young man kept offering, and then, finally, he gave up with a laugh. Willie didn't know why the stranger was laughing until he got home. The young man had been his oldest brother! He'd seen him so rarely, he hadn't recognized him!

But this stranger wasn't anybody's brother. Nobody knew him. That meant there was only one thing to do. The boys ran.

It took some time before the stranger, a former football player named Ron Thompson, was able to get them to listen to him. He was a softball coach, he explained. He'd been hurt playing football, and now he worked at coaching to stay close to sports. He had a regular softball team that was sponsored by the city of Detroit. He was inviting the boys to play with that team.

That first day they joined Thompson's softball team, Willie and his friends figured they'd just walk out onto the field and play ball. It didn't matter to Willie that there were white boys on the softball team. Back in Virginia, the Wolves were all white boys—except him. He hadn't even thought about white boys being "different," so he was startled when Thompson called all the boys on the team—black and white—together and told them that the first thing they were going to do that day was hug each other. They were a team. They were going to have to play that way, and so they were going to start out that way. If Willie was startled, it was even more of a shock for some of the white boys on the team. A lot of them had never been close to a person of a different race before.

Ron Thompson turned out to be a very, very special man. He was the first in a series of good men (after Pop) whom Willie one day would list as the people who meant most in his life. In later

RON THOMPSON. This picture of the man who coached Willie and the Ravens in both softball and football was taken many years later, when Thompson was coaching football at St. Martin de Porres High School. He had just been named Michigan State High School Coach of the Year. (Reprinted with permission from the *Detroit News.*)

DAMON KEITH. Judge Damon Keith was a young attorney when he first met Willie on the sandlots of Detroit. (Courtesy of the Walter P. Reuther Library, Wayne State University.)

years, Thompson became a legend in his own right, coaching football at De Porres High School. But for Willie and his friends, one of Thompson's greatest contributions was the way he made certain that the boys got to meet local high school coaches and other people who might help them and be role models for them. One of these men was Detroit Northwestern High School coach Sam Bishop. Willie knew about Northwestern. It seemed as though he knew about a lot of different schools in Detroit. He played softball with Thompson's team on the Poe school grounds. When they'd lived in the Avery apartment, he'd gone to school at Hancock Elementary school, over on Grand River Avenue. Now, because they were on Forest, he was in Jefferson Junior High. Northwestern was where boys in the projects went to school. It was supposed to be a really good place to go to school for a fellow who was interested in sports. Willie had already thought about that. If he used his sister's address, he'd be able to go to Northwestern High School, and that made meeting Coach Bishop serious business.

Bishop liked Willie on sight, too. Ron Thompson had told Bishop a few things about Willie—that his family didn't have much money (if any), that Willie was always in a good mood, and that he always tried his best. Bishop liked that. It was an important beginning to a very special friendship, and—right then— Bishop did something that would affect all the rest of Willie's life.

Sam Bishop introduced Coach Thompson's team to attorney Damon Keith. In the 1950s, there weren't that many black professionals in Detroit—but Damon Keith was recognized by both black and white Detroiters as someone that it was good to know. To Willie and his friends, Keith was something of a puzzle. Here was an African American who was genuinely successful. The boys in the projects were more used to seeing African Americans who were out of work—some of whom had reached the point where they no longer cared about anything at all. Bishop wanted the boys to see that success was possible and meet a real person who enjoyed that success.

The team was impressed by Damon Keith, all right—and Damon Keith? Keith was especially impressed by Willie Horton. Man and boy talked and talked that first day. The friendship they began would last for many years. Eventually, Damon Keith was introduced to Clinton Horton. If Damon Keith was impressed by Willie Horton, Clinton Horton was even more impressed by Damon Keith.

CHAPTER 3

"Keith is a man who oughtta be president—the first black president of the United States," Pop told Mom and Willie later.

FEDERATION BALL

Segregation was not the law in Detroit, but many things were segregated, just the same. Most of the people who lived in the projects were African American. White people, even poor white people, lived in different neighborhoods. Since they lived in different places, white children and black children went to different schools, played on different playgrounds, and went to different churches.

When people see each other as "different," all too often they find reasons not to get along. In Detroit, where black men and white men competed for the same factory jobs, a lot of African Americans didn't trust white Americans, and a lot of white people just plain didn't like black people much. Back in 1943, a riot had broken out. People roamed the streets fighting other people who were "different." Some people were killed. Now, ten years later, folks still remembered those days. The memory showed up in a lot of ways—including the city's recreation program.

Federation Baseball, which, in the 1950s, was Detroit's version of Little League ball, wouldn't let boys of different races play on the same team. Of course, the Federation still wanted to have good players of any race involved in their program. They just didn't believe in mixing people together. When they invited Coach Thompson's softball team to join the Federation, there was a small problem. Coach Thompson's team was racially mixed. It always had been. Convincing boys of different backgrounds that they could get along and play together was an important part of what Coach Thompson was trying to teach. If the softball team joined the Federation, the boys would have to be split up.

Splitting up the team was almost unthinkable. However, being part of the Federation would mean playing real baseball, not softball. Teams in the Federation had good sponsors, and good sponsors meant good equipment. There was an opportunity there for young players that couldn't be just shrugged off. Coach Thompson thought about it a long time. Finally, he thanked the Federation for their offer and promised that he'd ask his boys what they wanted to do.

"Nothin' doin'!!" "No way!" Every one of the boys shook his

head. "They're not splittin' us up. We're a team, and we stay that way!" The chorus of voices was loud and emphatic. Coach Thompson smiled. He was proud of the boys for having learned so much about people in the time they were together.

Willie and his friends would keep on playing softball one more year, but Coach Thompson didn't give up. He figured that there had to be a way to keep the team together and still play real baseball.

Thompson worked hard over the winter. He met with the city and with the Federation. He was determined to have it both ways: to keep his team together and to give them the advantages that came from playing in a league that was part of the Federation. He talked to managers and sponsors and all kinds of league officials. It took a long time, but finally, one morning, the people heading up the Billy Rogell League agreed that integrated baseball could have a chance.

So it was that, the following season, Willie Horton, future Detroit Tiger outfielder, caught for a team in the Billy Rogell League. Maybe the league name was prophetic. Billy Rogell had been a Detroit Tiger. He was the greatest shortstop the Tigers had ever had—up to that time.

⚾⚾⚾ **4** ⚾⚾⚾⚾

Boy Wonder

CLUBHOUSE BOY

Once he was playing Federation ball, it didn't take long before Willie attracted attention. He could hit a baseball just about as hard as he'd hit those bottle caps. His arm was good, too—so good that some of his teammates ducked when he threw the ball to them. Now that could be a problem! He was his team's number one catcher, and there were times when he had to fire the ball as hard as he could to second base to keep a runner from advancing. If the second baseman (or shortstop) ducked away . . . well, it certainly could be a problem. But Coach Thompson understood. Even for a player with a glove on, being on the receiving end of one of Willie's throws could hurt!

Willie thought baseball was just maybe the best game there ever was. But that was it. Baseball was a game, and growing up and earning money didn't have anything to do with it. Where baseball was concerned, Willie wanted to do his best; he wanted his team to win; he wanted to have fun—maybe not always in that order. Make money playing ball? That was for other people. But although Willie was just having fun, there was at least one man in Detroit who was doing some serious thinking about Willie and his place in baseball.

Detroit Tiger scout Lou D'Annunzio first spotted Willie when he was still playing softball for Coach Thompson. Every day during the summer, D'Annunzio's job was to spend long hours watching Detroit youngsters play ball. He knew how to tell which boys had a chance to make it on a professional team, and he earned his living by following those boys and watching them learn more and more about baseball. He reported on each boy's

37

progress, and, when the time was right, he'd recommend that his bosses sign the best of them to minor league contracts. After that, it was up to each player. If a boy kept on learning and improving, he might end up in the major leagues, where baseball history was made.

The year that Willie started to play Federation ball was the first year Detroit Tiger management heard his name. That year, Lou D'Annunzio reported to the club's director of scouting that there was a thirteen-year-old in the projects who had enough talent to make it all the way to the majors. D'Annunzio didn't say anything to Willie about making that report; it was far too soon to do that. But he kept watching him.

Baseball dominated summertime in Detroit—not just for Willie, but for everybody in town. People played baseball, talked baseball, and, when they could, they went down to the corner to watch the Tigers. Baseball was part of living. In the 1950s, watching the Tigers generally meant watching the Tigers get whipped, but Tiger losses didn't change the general atmosphere in town. Detroit loved baseball, and Detroit loved the home team. Willie was no exception.

He and his buddies loved to go to Tiger Stadium. It was called "Briggs Stadium" then, because most of it had been built when a man named Briggs owned the Tigers. They didn't have any money, so the boys had two choices if they wanted to see a game: wait until the late innings when the gates were open to everybody, or sneak in. Sneaking in could be done early, in time to watch batting practice.

Now batting practice is when you have the best chance to catch baseballs that come into the stands, and get autographs, and do all the things kids love to do in a ball park—so deciding whether to wait or try to get in early was pretty easy. Willie and his friends sneaked in. Sometimes they were successful. More often, they got caught.

It didn't have to be a game day for the boys to try to get into the ball park. Just watching practice was almost as good. Unfortunately, it was a lot easier to get caught sneaking in if there was no crowd there. One day, nabbed once again by a stadium guard, Willie and a friend pleaded not to be thrown out. They weren't very quiet about it, and all the ruckus caught the attention of a visiting Cleveland Indian outfielder named Rocky Colavito.

Rocco Domenico Colavito was a huge crowd-pleaser. A home

38

BRIGGS STADIUM. The cross-town freeways (I-96 and I-75) had not yet been completed when this picture was taken. Briggs Stadium nestles snugly at the corner of Michigan and Trumbull—the streets at the left and center of the photograph. The streets on the other two sides of the stadium are Cochrane (named for the great Tiger catcher-manager) and Cherry—which was later renamed in honor of Al Kaline. If you look carefully, at the very top of the picture you can see the footings of the Ambassador Bridge to Canada. Baseball was played at this corner for over a hundred years—from 1896 until 1999. (Courtesy of the Walter P. Reuther Library, Wayne State University.)

ROCKY COLAVITO. Rocco Domenico Colavito posed for this Tops baseball trading card in 1962, when he was a member of the Detroit Tigers. He looked exactly like this when, as a Cleveland Indian, he helped Willie and his friends get jobs working in the clubhouses at Briggs Stadium. (K. E. Bush collection.)

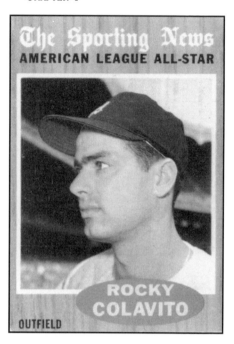

run hitter back when there weren't all that many people hitting the long ball, Rocky was as handsome as a movie star. He was a character, too. He had a whole series of "calisthenics"—stretching motions he went through each time he came up to bat. Women fans loved him. Men cheered the home runs. Kids twitched their hats, pulled up their belts, adjusted their sleeves, and put their bats across their shoulders to stretch—all because "the Rock" did it that way.

What a lot of people didn't know was that Rocky was very, very good with children. He insisted they be polite—he never signed an autograph until the young fan said "please," and he rarely gave it back before he heard a "thank you, Mr. Colavito"— but he genuinely liked kids. That day, he saw something in Willie that made him pay attention. "Oh, heck! Let the boys go," Rocky told the guard. "If they want in that badly, we'll find them something they can do."

Rocky took the pair to Rip Collins, the visiting clubhouse attendant. Collins managed the clubhouse where visiting ballplayers dressed and kept their equipment. Sure enough, between Rip and John Hand, who had the same job in the Tiger clubhouse, work aplenty was found for two very eager twelve-year-old boys. Willie and his buddy fetched water during batting and infield practice. They shined shoes. They ran errands. Best of all, they got to meet the Tigers and the visiting players.

The boys spoke to the players with respect. Willie had been taught to treat adults respectfully, anyway—and these men were something very special. After all, they were major league baseball players! Even when he was watching from the stands, Willie would never have called any of them by their first names. That wouldn't have been polite. At twelve or thirteen years old, Willie never, ever dreamed that some of those same major leaguers eventually would be his own teammates. Years later, he explained, "[Back then] I looked at ballplayers and they were God-given people. . . . I knew I could play baseball, but I thought [major leaguers] were special people."

For that matter, when Willie himself made the team in 1963, old habits died hard. It was still "Mr. Kaline" and "Mr. Phillips" and "Mr. Bunning" and "Mr. Foytack" and "Mr. Lary"—just as it had been in the days when he was running errands for them.

"For crying out loud, Willie!" Al Kaline once told him in exasperation. "Call me Al. You're part of the team, now!" Actually, if you count Rocky Colavito, who was traded to the Tigers in 1960, six of Willie's teammates when he first played in the major leagues were the very same men for whom he had run errands as a clubhouse boy.

A DIFFERENT SPORT

Stone Recreation Center stood at the corner of Forest and the John C. Lodge Freeway. Willie's home in the projects was on the north side, on Forest. The Lodge Freeway ran right past the east side of the projects. With a gym on his own street corner, it was only a matter of time before Willie wandered into it to try his hand at boxing.

It was Coach Thompson who introduced Willie to Martin Gilday, the coach at Stone Recreation. Gilday was quick to see that Willie had better than average boxing talent. Most of the trainers at the gym were equally impressed. Willie was the sort of athlete who, with a little work, could expect to have a career in boxing. To Willie, that sounded more than okay. Being stronger and faster and cleverer than an opponent in a boxing ring

41

CLINTON AND LILLIAN HORTON. Willie's parents were his best friends and his finest examples. Mom and Pop were strong people. Clinton Horton may have been poor, but his high standards, work ethic, and love for baseball were inspirations Willie would draw on for a lifetime. (Photo courtesy of Willie Horton.)

sounded like a pretty good way to make a living. He certainly was big enough to box, and strong enough, too. Gilday asked him how old he was. Willie thought quickly. If he admitted he was only thirteen, maybe they wouldn't let him box. "Sixteen," he said.

Willie thought a boxing career was a great idea, but Mom and Pop didn't agree—not one little bit. "Boxing is too risky, son," Pop told him. Mom was even more emphatic. Boxing was dangerous, Willie could get hurt, and he was going to stop boxing—NOW. That was all there was to it.

With both Mom and Pop against the idea, Willie didn't have much choice. It looked as if quitting was the only thing he could do. At least he had to make it look as if he had quit. He told his parents that he wouldn't box any more.

It wasn't very often that Willie crossed Mom and Pop, but this time he lied. He kept right on training for fights, sneaking in and out of the apartment and fibbing about where he was going or where he had been. If he'd thought about it at all, he might have realized that how he felt about boxing was a bit like how he felt

THE BROWN BOMBER. Willie's fascination with boxing never left him. Here, years after his own fling at the sport, he compares notes with another Detroit boxer, the one and only "Brown Bomber," Joe Louis. Louis stopped in the Tiger clubhouse to wish the team well during the 1968 pennant chase. (Courtesy of the Burton Historical Collection, Detroit Public Library.)

hitting those bottle caps. Boxing was something he could do well, and he just plain liked being able to do things well.

Unfortunately, it's hard to lie just one time about something. One big lie wouldn't have been quite so hard, but he had to keep on telling more and more little lies. The time came when Willie found himself smacked around pretty thoroughly in a fight. He came home with puffy eyes and a face full of bruises. Mom was worried, of course, and she was suspicious. Willie ducked his head.

"I'm really sorry, Mom," he said. "I got into a fight on the street. I know I should have walked away, but I didn't." At least the part about knowing he shouldn't have been fighting was true!

43

What actually blew the lid off his secret, though, was nothing short of a television program. Willie knew there was going to be a boxing tournament across the river from Detroit in Windsor, Ontario. It promised to be a good tournament with good competition, and Willie was eager to take part in it. He trained and trained and excitedly crossed the river to Canada to fight. The tournament was so important that it was covered by local newspapers, and the Canadian Broadcasting Corporation (CBC) broadcast most of the matches.

Willie had forgotten about Channel 9—the CBC television outlet in Detroit. When he got home the night after the tournament, he tried to sneak into the apartment. But both of his parents were sitting there waiting for him.

Though Pop didn't approve of boxing for Willie, he occasionally watched matches on television. He had been relaxing, watching the Windsor tournament, when, suddenly, he sat bolt upright. One of the boxers he was watching was his own teenage son! Not only that, his son was taking a licking. Man, oh, man! Willie was in trouble—BIG trouble. He was in trouble for boxing, but he was in a lot more trouble for lying.

"At least," said Pop, looking at Willie's bruised and puffy face, "you've not been seriously hurt yet. If you quit now—really quit—you're forgiven. But, remember, you've been very, very lucky to have boxed this long without doing yourself serious damage."

Willie promised, and this time he meant it. It wasn't really going to be that hard to keep his word, either. He hadn't been comfortable about lying—especially to his folks. And, after all, there was always baseball. Yep—from now on, baseball would be sport number one for Willie Horton.

THE RAVENS

The summer that Willie was fifteen, his Federation team joined a "Class E" amateur baseball league. Class E was a level above Federation ball, and it was made up of older boys who had spent a lot of time on the playing field. Being in Class E was a big step up. Class E still was amateur ball, but it was classed—measured in quality—using the same system that ranked the professional minor leagues. The very best minor league teams were "Triple-A," or AAA ball; the next best were called "Double-A," (AA). Then came A ball. The ranks continued through Class B, Class C, and Class D—on down to the lowly amateur teams in Class E. But once you were in Class E, you had your foot on the bottom rung of a ladder. People would be watching you, and it was possible that, one day, you would climb all the way up to the top.

Willie's team kept on playing three days a week in Federation games, but they also played two days a week in Class E. The team was still pretty much made up of the same boys who started out playing softball together for Coach Thompson, but now that they were Class E ballplayers, the team needed a proper name. "'Ravens' sounds good," somebody suggested—and "Ravens" it was.

Willie caught for the Ravens that year, just as he always had. He was hitting up a storm. In that first season in Class E ball, Willie's batting average was .470! Now it wasn't just Lou D'Annunzio watching him. Scouts from teams in both the American and National leagues were keeping an eye on this boy from the Detroit projects.

In baseball, teams like to think they are "strong up the middle." In other words, many baseball managers feel it is more important to find good catchers, good second basemen and shortstops, and good center fielders—players who can be found along the midline of a baseball diamond—than equally good athletes who play other positions. Players are "strong" if they can both field their positions and hit the ball well. When viewed in this light by the scouts, Willie was growing up to be a fairly strong catcher.

Willie was growing up in other ways, too. In the spring of 1958, he was to graduate from Jefferson Junior High School. He soon found that graduation was a mixed blessing. He was supposed to wear a suit for the graduation ceremonies. Willie had never owned a suit in his life. In Virginia and in the projects, blue jeans were about all anybody ever put on. But before he had much time to worry about how he could afford different clothes (the Horton family still had almost no money), Coach Thompson stepped in. Thompson's graduation present to Willie was a handsome business suit.

When September came around, it was time to enroll at Northwestern High School. Willie had been looking forward to playing for Northwestern's Coach Bishop ever since the day they had met at the Poe school grounds. Willie figured he could learn a lot from Sam Bishop.

Bishop was pleased to have Willie come to Northwestern, too. Not only was he sure that Willie would make a big contribution

45

NORTHWESTERN HIGH SCHOOL. The school fielded championship teams in a number of sports. Its dedication to baseball can be measured by all the diamonds that are part of the school grounds. This picture was taken in the 1920s, but the school and its grounds looked the same thirty years later, when Willie was playing ball for Sam Bishop. Walter P. Reuther Library, Wayne State University.)

to Northwestern sports, Sam Bishop saw a lot of himself in Willie Horton. He and Willie both had grown up in poor families; both of them loved all sports. Both had been taught from childhood that character and decency were more important than anything.

Bishop himself had dropped out of school when he was thirteen—a couple of years younger than Willie was now—to find work. Bishop was a promising athlete, and it wasn't long before "work" meant playing semiprofessional football. Eventually, he attracted the attention of a local high school coach, a man who recognized that there was a great deal more to Sam Bishop than could be seen on the playing field. He persuaded young Bishop to return to school. By then, Bishop was far older than his classmates, but he graduated from high school with honors and went on to college, where he was an excellent football player. He played college baseball, too, and he was an outstanding outfielder. After graduation, Bishop turned to coaching. It was a career choice that

SAM BISHOP. Sam Bishop was the legendary Northwestern High School coach whose dedication and example did much to influence the way that Willie grew up. Many professional sports figures passed through Bishop's hands, including baseball's Harry Chiti, Alex Johnson, and Hobie Landrith; football's Toby Arena, Henry Carr, Forest Evashevski, and Bill Kennedy; college coaches John Hackett and David Nelson; and boxing's Chuck Norris. (Courtesy of the Walter P. Reuther Library, Wayne State University.)

turned out to be a blessing for a great many young Detroit athletes—and for the entire world of sports.

When he looked at Willie Horton, Bishop was concerned. He and Willie had more in common than just their struggle against being poor. Willie wanted to play football. He had tried out for both the Northwestern baseball team and the Northwestern football team. Sam Bishop knew as well as anyone that hard-hitting football players courted injuries every day they were on the playing field. Football injuries could halt a baseball career, no matter how promising the player.

"You don't try to do both, Willie," Bishop told his new freshman. "You're a lot better in baseball than you are in football. You've got real baseball talent, and that talent can take you a long way. Don't risk it playing football. If you get hurt in football—and a lot of people do—you won't be able to play either game."

It was hard for Willie to take Coach Bishop seriously. He'd never play professional baseball anyway, so what did it matter if he got a little banged up playing football? It was all for fun.

Coach Bishop kept after him. He reminded Willie about how close Ron Thompson had come to making his way in professional sports, but that shoulder injury had stopped him. Finally, more or less convinced that football could be dangerous, Willie agreed to stay with just one sport—but he didn't agree with the part about his becoming a professional baseball player. That would never happen—no way!

For four years, until he graduated, Willie caught for the Northwestern High School baseball team. Studying wasn't Willie's favorite thing to do, but he stuck it out at school—mostly because Sam Bishop preached to him about that, too. Bishop knew all too well what it was like to be a high school dropout. He had been twenty-three years old—a grown man—when he finally received his diploma! He didn't want that to happen to Willie.

Willie listened to Coach Bishop—about school, about playing football, about everything. He did his best for his coach, but there was something at school (besides studying) that Willie didn't like very much. His schoolmates—and teammates too—teased him all the time about the way he was dressed.

Without money for new clothes, when Willie's old ones got torn, Mom mended them. If a tear was too big to sew together, she put a patch over it. When she could, she matched the patches to whatever it was that had a hole in it, but the patches weren't always of the same material. Sometimes there wasn't time for the tears to be mended, either, and so Willie came to school looking pretty tattered. And the other students laughed.

Sam Bishop saw what was going on. Quietly, he bought a set of new clothes and gave them to Willie. Then he found an after school job so that Willie could earn money to buy the rest of the things he needed.

Willie was stunned. "Boys my age don't cry," he told himself fiercely, but he was so grateful his throat ached anyway, and his eyes smarted. There wasn't any way to pay Coach Bishop back, but he could swear to stay in school. Bishop grinned. If Willie would stay in school, that was more than good enough payment for Sam Bishop. The two shook hands on it, and Willie went off to keep his promise.

A HIT AND AN ERROR

Mom and Pop were concerned about Willie for a different reason. Now that he was in high school, he was hanging with a different crowd. More than once, there had been a little trouble, and a stern policeman had arrived at the door with Willie in tow. It wasn't that he'd ever stolen anything. The only time Willie ever took something that didn't belong to him, it had cost him an entire summer baseball season. It wasn't likely that he'd ever do anything like that again!

"How the heck could stealing something cost you a baseball season?" one of his new friends asked. Willie didn't like remembering about it very much, but finally he explained. A couple of summers earlier, he had been in a Cunningham's drug store. He saw a baseball cap he liked. He didn't even think about it. He just took the cap, put it on his head, and wore it home.

"Where'd the hat come from, son?" Pop asked. "You been working for somebody?"

"No. I just got it at Cunningham's," replied Willie.

"What do you mean, you 'just got it'?" Pop said.

Willie explained. He liked the cap. He'd taken it.

The whipping Willie got that day lasted all the way from the apartment to the drug store. Once they reached the drug store, Pop made Willie promise the store manager that he would work all summer long for him—for free—to make up for taking that cap. Never mind that the cap was worth only $1.98. Never mind that the store owner was a Little League sponsor and really would much rather have had Willie out there catching for his baseball team. Willie had stolen, and Willie must pay—all summer long. And there went the baseball season.

No, it wasn't likely that Willie would ever steal anything again, but occasionally he turned up in the wrong place at the wrong time.

Actually, the police liked Willie. They knew he was basically a "good kid." Except for one time, they never took him to the station. When they found him doing something he shouldn't, they just scolded him, set him straight, and brought him home to Mom and Pop. Willie didn't dislike the policemen either. He figured they were a lot like his Pop. They weren't his enemies; they just wanted him to do better.

There was one time, though, when Willie ended up at the Vernor Street police station. A girl in the neighborhood was downright disrespectful to Mom, and that was something Willie wouldn't stand for. He told the girl what he thought, and then he found himself dealing with her two large and very disagreeable brothers. The fight got ugly. Somebody called the police, and Willie was hauled into the station lobby.

It was almost like the day he stole the baseball cap, only this time it was Coach Bishop who laid down the law. Willie was wearing a Northwestern jacket when he got in trouble, and he had disgraced the entire school—at least according to Sam Bishop. He didn't whip Willie; he slapped him—more than once. He punched him for emphasis while he yelled at him. He kept on yelling at him for quite a while, too. This was unacceptable behavior! This was going to stop!

Willie hung his head. He knew the coach was right; he knew the police were right; he knew he was in the wrong. It was going to stop, and it did.

THE LIGHT TOWER

Willie was sixteen years old and in the spring of his freshman year at Northwestern High School when he did something that had sports fans all across the city talking. Northwestern was paired against Cass Technical High School (better known as Cass Tech) in the 1959 Detroit Public School League championship game. The game was played at Briggs Stadium. Willie stood on the same playing field where he had worked as a clubhouse boy.

Northwestern was trailing in the middle innings when Willie came to bat against George Cojocari, ace pitcher for the Technicians. There were a couple of men on base—worth one, maybe two potential runs, if Willie could just get a hit. He dug in at the plate.

Cojocari set and pitched. "Ball one," said the umpire.

The pitcher looked over his shoulder to check his runners. With fewer than two out, they would be running on the pitch. He didn't want them to get any further off base than he could help. It was all right. Everybody was "holding;" no one was getting too big a lead. He pitched again. "Ball two."

Two balls and no strikes. Willie knew the pitcher wouldn't want to go to "three and oh," because then just one more pitch could walk the bases loaded. This next one was going to be right down the middle. He flexed his hands on the bat and then gripped it tightly.

Cojocari let go of the ball and Willie swung. He met the pitch perfectly—right on the "sweet spot"—and the ball took off. It was a high, fly ball, climbing up and up toward the right field seats. It kept climbing. While Willie stood there at home plate watching, the ball rose all the way out of the ball park, high over the upper deck in right field. At last it began to drop. It hit the base of a light

CAN YOU FIND WILLIE? The 1959 Northwestern High School baseball squad beat Cass Tech and won the city championship on the memorable night when Willie's home run hit the light tower at Briggs Stadium. Willie was fifteen years old, a high school freshman, at the time. Where is Willie? He's fourth from the left in the top row. The third player from the right in the same row is Willie's friend Alex Johnson, who also made it to the major leagues. (Reprinted from the *Norwester* with permission of Northwestern High School.)

tower, died, and rolled back onto the playing field. If it had missed the tower, it would have carried all the way to Trumbull Avenue.

Willie was scared to death. He didn't know a baseball could go that far.

As if from far away, he heard the umpire's voice. "Son, you've got to run the bases if you want that to be a home run." Willie turned toward first and broke into a trot.

As he circled the bases, the fans were still buzzing. This kid was a real wonder, all right. The only men who had ever hit balls over the roof in right field at Briggs Stadium during a game had been the great Ted Williams and Mickey Mantle, and both were batting lefthanded—naturally pulling the ball toward right field. Willie batted right-handed. When Willie sent a ball toward the right field roof, it was an "opposite field" home run. Willie hadn't even gotten all the way around on the ball, and still he'd smashed it off the light tower.

Northwestern went on to beat Cass Tech 13-10 and win the championship. The baseball scouts scribbled things in their notebooks.

⚾⚾⚾ **5** ⚾⚾⚾
From the Projects to Pro Ball

BONUS BABY

In the early 1960s, the excitement of playing for Class E baseball gave way to the stiffer competition and even greater excitement of playing in Class D. Willie was the star of the Class D Walways, and the other teams and other managers in the league spent a great deal of time wishing they had him on their side of the diamond.

Willie may have been a winner, but the Walway team was not. The team that headed for the Class D National Baseball Federation Tournament that year was one sponsored by Lundquist Insurance. But Willie wasn't left out. While his teammates had to cool their heels in Detroit, the Lundquist team invited Willie—and his bat—to go with them to Altoona, Pennsylvania, where the tournament was being played.

Getting to play in a national tournament was well beyond any of Willie's dreams. He couldn't believe his luck—and, not for the first time, he mentally blessed the people who were giving him the chance to play. He was scared to death that something could—something *would*—happen to mess everything up. There wasn't much he could do to control events, but he told himself that at least he'd get there plenty early to catch the team bus at Northwestern Field. He wasn't too sure how early "plenty early" was, but he wasn't about to take any chances. "You never know," he worried. "Maybe they'll change the time the bus leaves. Maybe there'll be some mixup. I'm not a regular Lundquist, so maybe they'll forget me!"

Just to be absolutely sure, Willie went to the field *four hours* before the bus was scheduled to leave. Scout Lou D'Annunzio was there early, too, but for D'Annunzio, "early" was an hour-and-a-half before the bus was supposed to load up. When he got to Northwestern, to his surprise, there sat Willie. It took D'Annunzio a little time to realize that Willie had been there, curled up on a bench sleeping, for a full two-and-a-half hours.

"Why?" D'Annunzio asked, astonished. "Did you think we'd leave you here?"

"I just wanted to be sure I didn't miss the bus," Willie grinned.

He didn't say any more than that, but he didn't need to. And Lou D'Annunzio didn't need words to understand that Willie was there early because he loved baseball and wanted to play. He was there early because he cared about doing the best he could. He was there early because he was the kind of player who would always do everything that was asked of him—and then a little bit more. D'Annunzio nodded to himself. Sometimes he second-guessed himself when he pulled young players out of the crowd, but with Willie he was sure he had picked a winner. D'Annunzio kept on smiling, and Willie went on to Altoona and hit .600 in the tournament—doing far more than his share to ensure that Lundquist Insurance came home with the national championship.

Happy as he was with Willie's progress, D'Annunzio was getting a little nervous. Willie attracted a lot of attention, and not all of it came from the Detroit Tigers. By the end of his freshman year in high school, Willie was receiving contract offers from any number of major league teams. Coach Sam Bishop was concerned about it, too, though for a different reason.

Willie wasn't experienced in business, and—no matter how much fans and players may love it—baseball is a business. Willie had no defense if a club tried to sign him for less money than he was worth. For that matter, he had never handled money of any kind—not in quantity. He wouldn't know what to ask for during contract negotiations. He had no idea what, besides baseball and money, should be a part of an agreement between player and club.

Knowing that Willie and attorney Damon Keith already were good friends, Bishop talked to Pop. It probably would be a good idea, he said, if Pop talked to Damon Keith about being both Willie's agent and his legal guardian. Keith then could be responsible for helping Willie negotiate any contract that was offered him. Pop nodded. It made very good sense. Assisting in negotiations was a normal role for an attorney, and since Damon Keith knew Willie so well, he'd understand—without prompting—what kinds of spe-

LOU D'ANNUNZIO. Lou D'Annunzio was a Tigers' scout for many years—working first from Dearborn, Michigan, and later from his retirement home in Titusville, Florida. He spotted Willie on the Detroit sandlots, and his determination was a major reason that Willie signed with the Tigers and not some other team. (Courtesy of the Walter P. Reuther Library, Wayne State University.)

cial offers would be really meaningful for Willie and his family. Finally, as a "legal guardian," Keith could continue overseeing Willie's financial interests as long as it was necessary. It made good sense to everybody else, but, at first, Willie wasn't so sure.

"You're not giving me away, are you?" he asked Pop worriedly. Pop grinned in exasperation at his son. As if there was any chance of *that!*

Although the Tigers weren't the only club who wanted to sign Willie Horton, thanks to information given them by Lou D'Annunzio, they knew best what kind of offer it would take to get Willie's attention. And, while Tiger officials were preparing to talk contract, D'Annunzio stayed close to Willie. The amount of time a scout spent with a prospect usually had a lot to do with which club got to sign that prospect. Willie's family knew and trusted Lou D'Annunzio, and D'Annunzio saw to it that they continued to feel that way.

At the time the Tigers were hoping to sign Willie to his rookie contract, Willie's father didn't have a job—not even a part-time one. He *couldn't* work. Clinton Horton had been "on disability" for some time. Disability payments represented even less money than he'd been able to bring home when he was working part-time jobs.

Ultimately, Pop's inability to earn money for his family

SIGNED BY THE TIGERS. It's official! Seated in General Manager Rick Ferrell's office, Willie signs the contract that makes him a Detroit Tiger. Damon Keith stands at the left of the picture, and a very happy (and relieved) Lou D'Annunzio is at the right. Willie is wearing the suit that Ron Thompson gave him. (Reprinted with permission from the *Detroit News*.)

helped the Tigers and Willie get together sooner than they might have done otherwise. Knowing that something had to be done for Willie's family gave the Tigers some idea what they would have to put into any contract to get Willie to sign it. But "doing something for Willie's family" affected the timing of the contract, too. High school juniors are not supposed to sign major league contracts unless there is some kind of financial hardship involved. Willie definitely qualified for a "hardship clause." It was simple: if Clinton Horton wasn't working, Willie was the breadwinner for his family. He could earn money playing baseball, but the Tigers couldn't pay him anything unless they signed him. Invoking a hardship clause made everything possible.

On August 7, 1961, Willie took the elevator to the second floor of the small office building attached to Briggs Stadium. He got out, walked past the ticket department, and went down a narrow hall into General Manager Rick Ferrell's office. There he sat down at a conference table and put his name on a piece of paper. He was just eighteen years old, but he was a Detroit Tiger.

Right up until the last minute—even in the car on the way to the ball park—Willie thought that he was going to sign with the New York Yankees. The Yankees had sent him a catcher's mitt, after all—and they hadn't backed off, even when they knew the Tigers were close to signing him. Pop and Damon Keith knew better. When they got to Tiger Stadium, they turned to Willie. "This is where we're stoppin,'" Pop said.

Lou D'Annunzio beamed—in relief, as much as in pride. Willie Horton was one rookie ballplayer he was very, very glad he hadn't lost to another team—especially to the hated Damnyankees!

Willie was so happy he couldn't believe it. He had money. He had a job playing baseball—the thing he did better than anything else in the whole world. And maybe the best thing of all was that Mom and Pop wouldn't have to live in the projects any more.

Mom wanted a great big house—the bigger the better. She wanted to be able to have all the children and grandchildren around her at the same time. The real estate agents showed her smaller houses, but Mom was firm. Yes, most of the time she and Pop would be there all alone, but there still had to be room for everybody. What about Christmas? What about birthdays?

Mom finally settled on a house in north-central Detroit that once belonged to automaker Henry Ford. It was the third house Ford had lived in during the time he was becoming one of the

RICK FERRELL. During forty years in the Detroit Tigers' front office, Hall of Fame catcher Rick Ferrell was involved in the signing of many of the team's greatest players. This picture was taken in 1987, but Rick looked much the same the day in 1961 when he gave Willie Horton a $50,000 bonus for signing with the team. (Photo courtesy of Kerrie Ferrell.)

world's greatest auto manufacturers. It certainly had plenty of bedrooms! Of course, houses that large are expensive to keep up, but as part of their contract with Willie, the Tigers worked out a deal with the utility people so that Mom and Pop wouldn't have to worry about the cost of gas and electricity.

The Tigers bought Willie a new car, too—his first car. It was a Pontiac Bonneville. He loved it. It was great just driving it around town—or it was great until the day he got the paint a little skinned up. Pop put his foot down—hard. "You don't need no car," he said. "The next car you get, you be twenty-one, and you buy it for yourself." And Pop sold the Bonneville! He had it repaired, and then it was gone. If Willie wasn't mature enough to drive like a grown-up, he wasn't going to have a car until he was an adult and legally independent.

When the Tigers signed Willie, he was what baseball calls a "bonus baby." In addition to an annual salary, he was given $50,000 just for signing the contract. In 1961, that was about ten times as much money as the average person earned in a whole year.

Willie was thinking about all the things he could buy with the money, but Damon Keith shook his head. That much money all at once wasn't for spending. It was for investing. Willie's bonus would be put to work so it could grow and turn into even more money in the future. And part of it had to go toward a down pay-

SAM BISHOP'S MAN. In 1962, the year Willie graduated from high school, he was already Detroit Tiger property. That year the *Norwester* (the Northwestern High School Yearbook) was dedicated to Coach Sam Bishop and the many professional athletes he had trained. The yearbook proudly allotted Willie his own full page. (Reprinted from the *Norwester* with permission of Northwestern High School.)

ment on the house. Out of his $50,000 bonus, Willie ended up with only about a hundred dollars in spending money, but it didn't really matter. He still was the happiest he had ever been in his life.

There was one complication associated with being a professional ballplayer. Willie would have to miss some school. There was no way around it, although he wouldn't miss any more than could be helped. About school, the Tigers agreed completely with Coach Sam Bishop and Willie's other advisors. Baseball careers didn't last forever. Graduating from high school and having a diploma were very, very important—not just for education's sake, but so that Willie would have that diploma when the time came for him to take a job outside of baseball. Willie's playing assignments must not keep him from graduating from Northwestern High School.

As it turned out, when he graduated in 1962, Willie was behind his old classmates by less than half a semester.

ꑷꑷꑷ **6** ꑷꑷꑷ

Making It in the Minors

THE MINOR LEAGUES

Bob Sullivan had scouted for the Tigers for a good many years, spending season after season scouring western Michigan for baseball talent—doing much the same kind of thing that Lou D'Annunzio did in Detroit. Almost more important, however, Sullivan was the organizer and driving force behind the Grand Rapids, Michigan, Sullivans.

The Sullivans were an independent baseball club—not affiliated with any major league team—but they were the training ground for a surprising number of young major league players. Almost every season, the Sullivans could be counted on to field a quantity of professional and semiprofessional athletes. Some of these were rookies—youngsters just starting out in the game. Others were baseball's "old men" of thirty and thirty-five who had slowed down enough that they no longer could play regularly in the major leagues. With veteran players on the team, the Sullivans were a great place for rookies to pick up the kind of discipline required in the major leagues. So once he was safely signed, the Tigers sent Willie off to Grand Rapids to play out the summer season with the Sullivans—and to learn to be an outfielder.

The year before Willie signed with the Tigers, the team had signed the Federation's star catcher, Bill Freehan, to a contract with a huge bonus—$100,000. The Tigers really didn't need another rookie behind the plate. Freehan was outstanding at the position, and it was the only position he played. Tiger General Manager Rick Ferrell (former All Star and soon to be Hall of Fame catcher) read the scouting reports carefully and talked to Lou D'Annunzio. D'Annunzio had paid close attention to the way

61

Willie moved around the plate. He'd checked to see how quickly he could get under foul fly balls and pop-ups. He'd looked at the accuracy and speed of Willie's throws to the infield. He'd listened as Willie talked to his pitchers. In amateur and semipro ball, the manager generally decided what pitches would be thrown, but a catcher still needed to have an idea how to handle pitchers and call a game.

D'Annunzio knew Willie was a very good catcher, but he also knew that Willie had a lot of potential as an outfielder. When Willie had taken that trip to Altoona with the Lundquist team as an "extra man," the Lundquists already had a catcher—none other than a fellow from Royal Oak, Michigan, named Bill Freehan! That time, Willie had volunteered to move to the outfield so Freehan could catch. (Willie was the first to congratulate Bill, too—when Freehan was named the Most Valuable Player in the game.) Yes, Willie could make a top-flight outfielder if he worked at it—and the Tigers would see to it that he had the chance to work at it.

Willie finished the summer season swinging the bat hard and getting more than his share of hits—and trying to learn not to be a catcher any more.

Willie was officially Tiger property, so his baseball season didn't end once the Sullivans' season was over. He was about to discover "winter ball."

In the south of Florida, as well as in Central and South America, the weather is warm in December and January, and so baseball is played all year long. Rookies get sent to "winter ball" as a kind of baseball school—one where the teams that signed them can watch them grow and develop as players. Seasoned players occasionally play winter ball too, because spending days in the hot sun makes it easier to recover from injuries. There were more veteran ballplayers in winter ball in Willie's day than there would be in later years, because in 1960 more sophisticated ways to rehabilitate weren't available. Also, in that time before multi-million dollar salaries, veterans sometimes played just because winter ball is a source of off-season income.

Regardless of the baseball era, more often than not, rookies end up playing in the Florida Instructional League. This is a league where teams are managed and coached by men who are

BOB SULLIVAN. Tiger scout Bob Sullivan organized the Grand Rapids Sullivans, the semipro team to which Willie was sent after he was signed by the Tigers. (Courtesy of the Walter P. Reuther Library, Wayne State University.)

picked for their ability to help young athletes improve their playing skills. Florida can be a particularly good place to be for a rookie who is learning a new field position, and in 1960, Willie needed all the practice he could get. Later he would tell people that it took him nearly eight years to stop "throwing like a catcher."

Willie knew he had been sent to Tampa, Florida, that winter of 1961 so the coaches there could turn him into an outfielder, but he still had a surprise waiting for him when he arrived. He expected to take his glove out onto the field and play ball, just as he always had done, but in Tampa nobody seemed to care whether he got into a game or not. Everything was focused on teaching him to play the outfield—not just how to catch and field, but where to throw the ball after he caught it, how to play the batters, and how to work with the other outfielders so that they wouldn't slam into each other when they were running after the ball.

All during that first winter, Willie came to bat just one time. He shagged a lot of flies during practice (that is, he caught balls hit by men working on their batting swings) and practiced his throws, but during the games he sat on the bench—in baseball slang, just "gathering splinters." He also spent an awful lot of

PHIL CAVARETTA. When Willie first reported to play winter ball, he found himself babysitting for the manager's young son, Corky. Here Corky's dad, Phil Cavaretta, gives Willie some pointers on his batting stance. (Reprinted with permission from the *Detroit News.*)

time keeping an eye on Coach Phil Cavaretta's young son, Corky. There were days that he felt a lot more like a baby-sitter than a professional ballplayer.

But Willie was determined to use his time well. While he sat on the bench, he asked questions, and he paid attention to the answers. He learned from his coaches; he learned from his team-mates. And he made new friends. One player in particular, Gates Brown, would be his close friend for years and years and years to come.

Willie had a lot to think about besides baseball during that winter. Technically, he was still a junior in high school. He'd worked hard during the fall, wanting to complete as many classes as he could between the Sullivans' season and his departure for Florida. But that wasn't all. It wasn't just school and baseball, Willie had something else very important on his mind.

With three years on the Northwestern team, Willie was a school baseball hero long before he signed with the Tigers. As a result, a Northwestern girl named Patricia Strickland was asked to interview Willie for the school newspaper. "Who's Willie Horton?" Patricia asked disinterestedly—and went on to do a different interview, instead. She didn't find out "who Willie Horton was" until several months later when she and Willie met at a school prom. Then, she learned a great deal, and she liked what she learned—a whole lot. And Willie certainly liked Patricia!

When Willie left to play Instructional League ball in Tampa, he was thinking about Patricia. At Christmastime, there was a break in play, and Willie came back to Detroit. He and Patricia were married in 1961, just one week before Christmas—so when Willie headed back to Florida, he was a married man. Being a husband still felt very "new" when February came along, and it was time for spring training with all the rest of the Detroit Tigers.

⚾⚾⚾⚾⚾

The Tigers said they wanted to make an outfielder out of Willie, but as he looked around Lakeland's Henley Field that spring, Willie wasn't so sure about the plan. The Tigers had a solid outfield already, with Al Kaline in right, Billy Bruton in center, and Rocky Colavito in left. It would be a long while, he thought, before they needed a rookie like him. For that matter, the whole Tiger team was good—and none of the players was very old—well, not old except for Billy Bruton. Billy's uniform number was 38, and a lot of people kidded that he wore his age on his back!

Still, spring training 1962 was an exciting time to be a Tiger. The 1961 Tigers, under manager Bob Scheffing, had won a record 101 of their 162 games. Had it not been for a disastrous September, the Tigers would have beaten the mighty New York Yankees and gone on to play in the World Series. Detroit fans, the same ones who had managed to keep on loving the slumping Tigers all through the 1950s, went nuts over the '61 team. No longer did sports editorial cartoons show a Tiger tail sticking up out of a manhole (a long-running joke that the Tigers spent all their time in the sewers—the "basement" of the American

League). In 1961 the Tigers roared, and Detroiters cheered them on, filling the ball park game after game. Even *Life* magazine ran a huge photo spread on the team as it stayed "one-two" (in first or second place) and challenged the mighty Yankees. Who knew what would happen in the new 1962 season?

For Willie, what would happen in 1962 was Class C ball. He was a rookie, he needed seasoning, and the Tigers sent him to their Northern League affiliate in Minnesota—the Duluth-Superior Dukes.

It's not unusual for a rookie, even a top prospect, to have fairly poor numbers the first season in the minor leagues. There are so many things to adjust to, so many different people, so many management styles, and—in Willie's case—a whole new position to play. The Tigers probably expected Willie to hit about .260 at Duluth, at best—and they wouldn't have worried if he had, at least not if he appeared to be improving toward the end of the season and looked good the following spring.

Willie was 'way ahead of that program. He hit a solid .295 with the Dukes. He had fifteen home runs and a very respectable seventy-two runs batted in (R.B.I.'s). That last number proved he could hit when it was most important—with men on base. Rick Ferrell looked at the big board in his office that tracked all the ballplayers who belonged to the Tigers, regardless of where they played, and he smiled—the same contented smile Lou D'Annunzio had worn the day Willie signed his contract.

At the end of the Duluth season, Willie was "pumped." He could hardly wait for spring training the following year. There still were classes to take at Northwestern, but Willie thought mostly about baseball and more baseball. He and Pat moved in with Mom and Pop—there certainly was room enough—and he spent long hours in the basement, just swinging his bat at imaginary pitches. "What on earth are you doing down there all by yourself, Willie?" Patricia would call. And Willie tried to explain.

He was trying to level out his swing and work on bat speed. If he worked at it, he could keep his motion smooth and practice turning his hands over quickly as he swung. If he did that, the bat would pick up speed as it crossed the plate. He could try to be sure there was no hitch in his swing—that he didn't pull the bat backward when it should have begun its movement forward. He could do all that without anybody else there. Pat didn't quite understand yet, but she knew her husband was determined to do the best he could. She figured the Tigers would like his *trying*, at least!

Once again, Willie went to Florida for winter ball—this time to Dunedin. In the winter of 1962–1963, he had an extra reason to play hard, too. Young Darryl William Horton had been born to Willie and Patricia on October 10, 1962.

Willie was still doing his best and more besides (giving 200 percent, the coaches said) in spring training. He finally was adjusting to outfield play, and, even more important, he never minded working hard on any area where his game was less than perfect.

Tiger officials watched Willie very carefully. They were more concerned with their starting outfield than they had let on to the press. It wasn't just Billy Bruton's age that bothered them. Rocky Colavito's home run total was down, and that year even Al Kaline was slumping slightly. The Tigers needed outfield "insurance." That meant that Willie needed to be as close to the major leagues as they could get him.

At the beginning of that year, the Tigers had reorganized their minor leagues. Duluth was reclassified, moving from Class C to Class A. Knoxville, Tennessee, which had been the club's only Class A team, now was Class Double-A (AA), and there was a new Triple-A club in Syracuse, New York. Whether Duluth was Class C or Class A, a move from there to Syracuse was a huge jump—but in the spring of 1963, the Tigers sent Willie to Syracuse to play with the Chiefs. As a Chief, Willie was just one level below the majors.

Willie lasted about three weeks in Syracuse. He kept on trying hard to be the best he could be, but now he tried too hard. In baseball, when a player works so hard at something that the trying gets in the way of the doing, it's called "pressing." Willie was pressing—big time. Figuring he'd get discouraged if his struggle went on too long, the Tigers acted quickly: After playing just twenty-one games in Syracuse, Willie found himself with the Tigers' Double-A club in Knoxville, in the Sally League.

For Willie, it would have been tough to say which was harder to take—the continuing struggle at Syracuse (he'd hit only .218 against Triple-A pitching) or being demoted to Double-A. He felt sure he had failed miserably. His managers said all the right things. Patricia tried to talk to him, but Patricia was one of the people he felt he'd let down. For that matter, he'd let everybody down, including himself—or so Willie thought. Finally, he called Pop.

"Hey, it's just a slump," Pop told him—and the confidence in his voice was almost as good to hear as what he was saying.

"You're just in a slump. Go ahead and play the way you know you can play. Don't matter what field you're on. You can play in Tennessee just as easy as you can in New York. Don't worry about it. Every ballplayer in the world has slumps, and you can bet the Tigers know that, too."

It was good advice, and better yet to hear it coming from Pop. So Willie was just in a slump. Well, the way out of a slump was to go play ball—not that there had been any choice whether he would or not. But now Willie felt a little better about everything.

The Knoxville Smokies were a Double-A team—a notch above Duluth, so the Tigers must think he was a better player than he'd been last year. That was great, because in Duluth he'd already been pretty good. Here in Knoxville the players were a little younger than they'd been in Syracuse, and the pace of the game was a little easier than it was in Triple-A. The pitching was a whole lot easier to handle. The Knoxville Smokies included a lot of Willie's friends, too—fellows he had played with in Florida. With Willie on the field, the Knoxville outfield was made up of Willie Horton, Mickey Stanley, and Jim Northrup. Willie didn't know it in 1963, but in just five years' time, that entire outfield would be part of the 1968 World Champion Detroit Tigers team.

Willie hit .333 in Knoxville. He socked fourteen home runs for the season and had seventy R.B.I.'s—a record comparable to the one he'd had the previous year in a much weaker league—and he'd done it even though he'd missed the first few weeks of the season. (The time spent in Syracuse didn't count toward Knoxville statistics.) Pop had been right. Willie held his head high. He didn't exactly forget his struggle in Syracuse, but he was a happy man.

The Tigers were pleased, too. When the minor league season ended on the first of September, Willie was called up to Detroit. He would finish out the year with the parent club. It was traditional for managers to use September to take a look at promising rookies in a major league setting. All the teams did that, but the Tigers were particularly interested in looking at Willie.

Early in the 1963 season, the Tigers had made some front office changes. Jim Campbell, who up until then had been vice president and director of minor league operations and scouting, now was named the Tigers vice president and general manager. That was what Rick Ferrell had been when he signed Willie (actually, vice president and director of major league personnel). Ferrell was still there, but after the reorganization, his title was

JIM CAMPBELL. Jim Campbell's appointment as general manager of the Detroit Tigers set a number of things in motion that dramatically changed Willie's world. Not only was Campbell responsible for bringing in manager Charlie Dressen—who was like a second father to Willie—Campbell himself became one of the most important men in Willie's life. (Reprinted with permission from the *Detroit News.*)

just vice president. No longer burdened by the general manager's duties, he would be able to do more to support scouting and player development.

In June of 1963, Jim Campbell began to do things the way he personally felt they should be done. He changed field managers. Popular skipper Bob Scheffing was fired—something that can happen even to the best of managers when their teams don't win. And after the wonder year of 1961, Scheffing's 1962 and 1963 teams had looked ordinary. In his place, Campbell brought in former Brooklyn Dodger manager Charlie Dressen.

A peppery little man, Dressen had a reputation for making things happen. He was good at building teams, and he liked working with young players. Dressen knew that Campbell expected him to build the Tigers into something even better than the team they had been two years before, and he was worried about his outfield. Rocky Colavito's home run total, which dropped from forty-five in 1961 to thirty-seven in 1962, was just twenty in September of 1963. (He'd finish the year with twenty-two homers). Billy Bruton's numbers were down, too. The only man Dressen could count on at all was Al Kaline. He wanted to take a really good look at this Willie Horton he'd been hearing about.

And Willie gave Dressen something to see. Willie played fifteen games with the Tigers that September. His very first major league at bat came when the Tigers were in Washington, D.C., playing the Senators. "I'll never forget that first game," he said later. "It was about the fifth inning when I came into the dugout in uniform. I hardly had time to say hello to anybody when Charlie Dressen said, 'Can you hit?' I said I could, and he said, 'Well, get up there and hit.' I thought he was teasing me. . . . When I realized he was serious and wanted me to pinch-hit for the pitcher I hardly even had time to be scared. I just went up there and got a hit."

Willie faced Senator pitcher Jim Hannan, took a couple of pitches, and then hit the ball hard. It bounced through the infield for a clean single—a solid hit, the very first time he tried! The runner on base scampered home. Willie had tied the game in his very first major league at bat!

The next time Willie came to bat for the Tigers, they were back home in Tiger Stadium (Briggs Stadium had been renamed Tiger Stadium in 1960, when the Briggs family sold the team to John Fetzer). This was a place Willie knew. He'd played there before—that time in 1959 when he put the ball almost all the way out of the park.

In his second Tiger at bat, pinch-hitting again, Willie faced Robin Roberts, ace Oriole pitcher and future Hall of Famer. He hit the very first pitch Roberts threw him, and it sailed far into the upper deck in left field for a long home run!

Robin Roberts, who had gone to school at Michigan State University, was one of Willie's heroes. Willie got the ball back. (In those days, baseball fans usually didn't mind trading a home run ball for a different baseball, once they understood why the hitter wanted it back.) He took the ball to Roberts and asked him to autograph it. "He musta thought I was crazy," Willie laughed as he told reporters about it years later.

Charlie Dressen had seen enough. During the rest of the season, Willie was in the regular lineup. In fifteen games, he came to bat forty-three times and hit for a very respectable average—.324.

⚾⚾⚾ 7 ⚾⚾⚾
Almost a Major Leaguer

THE BOYS FROM SYRACUSE

The spring training radio announcers stared at each other in confusion. Fans at home listened as each broadcaster asked the other the same questions over and over. "What was THAT?" "Did he hit it?" "Did he swing?" "What happened?" "No, he checked his swing." "There's a piece of the bat over there. . . ." "Yeah, I think he checked his swing." "Did the pitcher drill him? Did the pitch hit the bat?"

That day in spring training, Willie had just done something that had the Tigers and their fans scratching their heads. He came up to bat, started to swing at a pitch, decided he didn't like it, and so he checked his swing. That was nothing special; batters are allowed to change their minds about swinging at a pitch. Checked swings are part of baseball. The batter has to stop his swing in a hurry, though. If the fat part of the bat crosses over the center of home plate, it counts as a strike whether he wants to swing or not.

Willie checked his swing in a hurry—but he had started it with so much force, and he checked it so suddenly, that his bat snapped right in half! The barrel of the bat bounced up the third base line as the announcers and everybody on the field stared at it in astonishment.

No one could remember such a thing happening before. Bats break, of course, but not by themselves. If the batter hits the ball just wrong (or just right, depending on the point of view), the bat can shatter. But a bat had never broken all by itself until Willie showed what could happen if the batter was strong enough and swinging hard enough.

THE SWING OF THE BAT. Willie could swing a bat harder than just about anyone else. Here he completes his swing in the batting cage and looks to see how cleanly he has hit the ball. (Courtesy of the Burton Historical Collection, Detroit Public Library.)

It had taken some time for the newspapers to realize that Willie was a "power hitter"—someone who could be counted on to hit the long ball. He was strong, and his home runs were long ones, but for some reason the papers didn't pick it up. When he broke a bat without even hitting the ball, his image began to change.

Early in spring training, Charlie Dressen repeatedly compared Willie to the great Dodger catcher, Roy Campanella. The newspapers agreed and happily told the fans at home that their new young Tiger had the same strength and the same build as Campy—and he could hit for average. Now reporters began to admit that Willie hit home runs, too—and that he'd hit a lot more of them just as soon as he had figured out how to handle major league pitching.

⚾⚾⚾⚾⚾

During the winter of 1963–1964, Willie worked in construction. It was something he could do to bring in money, and the heavy work helped keep him in shape—at least while he was doing it. Maybe all that bending and lifting caused him to work up an extra big appetite. Whatever the reason, when he met his friend Gates Brown that spring (the two had planned to drive together to Florida for spring training), they worked their way very, very slowly through West Virginia—eating as they went. Between friends who were ready to feed them and restaurants full of good southern home cooking, Willie was in heaven. He loved food. He probably loved it a little too much, for when he and "the Gater" reported to spring training, both men were well over their playing weights—Willie by twenty-two pounds.

This was the spring that Charlie Dressen expected Willie to begin his major league career, and he was not happy when he got a look at Willie's extra poundage. Dressen didn't want his players using spring training time to get into shape. They were supposed to arrive in camp that way, especially when they had as much work to do in the field as Willie did. Dressen laid down the law. There would be a $100 fine for each pound of the twenty-two that Willie failed to lose over the next two weeks.

Frantically, Willie dieted and exercised, far too fast and too hard for it to be considered a healthy way to lose weight, but he got those twenty-two pounds off in a hurry. Proudly, he weighed in at the clubhouse at the end of the two weeks, and Charlie Dressen grinned at him.

Willie was puzzled. Reporters were gathered around, and there even was a photographer. Surely losing a little weight wasn't worth all that attention! Dressen had that impish grin of his working big time. He disappeared for a minute and came back with a huge package in his arms. He was holding a twenty-two pound ham!

"That's how much weight you took off, Willie," the manager said. "Now, don't eat the whole ham at one time! Here. Let me show you how to cook it." (Dressen had quite a reputation as a cook.) Willie collapsed in laughter. He certainly never expected anything like that ham!

That spring, Willie and Charlie Dressen were close and getting closer, each respecting the other as a man as well as player and manager. Dressen liked what he saw in Willie from the start—his attitude, his willingness to work on things he didn't do well, his physical strength, and his raw talent. The comparisons to Roy Campanella weren't made just for the sake of the newspaper writers who needed something to put in their columns. Dressen meant every word—and he was determined to make Willie live up to what he saw in him.

Unfortunately, 1964 wouldn't be the only season that Willie reported in overweight at the beginning of the baseball year. Willie's weight was a chronic problem. "Take it off now and keep it off," Dressen warned him. "When you get old like me, you won't be able to lose it."

But it wasn't just Willie's weight that Dressen fussed about. He made Willie into a special project. He monitored his progress on the field, encouraged his hitting, and talked with him for hours about things that happened off and on the field. Willie felt as if he'd somehow acquired a second father.

Back home in Detroit, Pop wasn't jealous at all. He was so proud of Willie—so glad he had raised the kind of son that a man like Charlie Dressen would think was worth helping. When Willie came north with the Tigers as a regular member of the team, Clinton Horton was fairly glowing. Pop loved baseball, and he couldn't think of anything better in the world than to sit in the middle of the bleachers at Tiger Stadium and watch his son holding down left field.

There was a little bit of a question about those bleacher seats. Clinton had always sat there. "I've always liked the bleachers best," he insisted. But a lot of people felt that the father of one of the players should sit in a better seat. In fact, the Tigers had

WILLIE, CHARLIE DRESSEN, AND THE TWENTY-TWO POUND HAM. Willie's battle with his weight would be a factor throughout his career, but he never lost weight more dramatically—nor was rewarded more spectacularly—than the spring training when he lost twenty-two pounds and was given a twenty-two pound ham as a prize for doing so. Manager Charlie Dressen, shown here holding the famous ham, offered to help Willie cook it. (Reproduced with permission from AP/Wide World Photos.)

reserved several rows behind and above the home team dugout, and player families usually sat there to watch the games. But not Pop. Pop stayed out there in the bleachers, pointing proudly to Willie and telling everybody who would listen, "That's my boy!"

Willie started the 1964 season in left field, with Billy Bruton in center and Al Kaline in right. He thought he'd known about pressure before. Every time he walked out onto the playing field, he put pressure on himself to do his best. But pressure in the major leagues was different.

He knew that Pop was there watching. He knew that Charlie Dressen believed in him. He knew he had a lot to learn, and he tried to listen to the coaches who were there to help him. He listened to the advice that Billy Bruton and his old friend Gates Brown gave him, too. He worked so hard on his outfield play that he couldn't concentrate on his hitting. Then the coaches talked to him about his swing and ways he could improve his batting average. Willie's head was spinning.

It wasn't that he was afraid he couldn't do better. He knew he could. His hitting had been good in Knoxville and Duluth, but that was against minor league pitching. In the majors he needed different skills. He kept on working hard, and then he worked harder. It was just like it had been during those first twenty-one games in Syracuse in 1963. He was pressing. The more he tried to fix something, the worse everything got.

Willie knew he wasn't as strong as he should be, either. Losing all that weight so fast bothered him more than he had realized. That was part of the problem, and so was the fact that pressure to succeed was coming from so many directions at once. His luck didn't help much, either. Even dumb things got in his way. One day Gates Brown was using a scalpel (a razor sharp surgical knife) to make slits in the sides of his playing shoes. A lot of players did that. It let their toes spread out and made the shoes more comfortable. Willie walked up behind Gater and tapped him on the shoulder in greeting. Gater, startled because he hadn't known Willie was coming, jumped. He forgot that the scalpel was still in his hand. Willie ended up with three stitches in his finger and several days when he couldn't hold a bat.

Willie hung in for twenty-five games. It was almost a relief when he was sent back to the minor leagues—but not to Knoxville this time. This time it was understood that Willie was major league material, and the minor league assignment was temporary. He'd go to Syracuse, get some practice playing with other men who were almost ready for the major leagues, and he'd be back in Detroit before he knew it! At least that's what Charlie Dressen told him. And that move more or less established the "boys from Syracuse" who would make such a difference in the Tigers 1968 season.

Major league ballplayers have to come from somewhere. Of course, many clubs trade for established ballplayers to improve their teams. Baseball is set up in such a way that there are certain months when players can and can't be traded—that is, swapped from one team to another. Sometimes a team that needs a veteran player as an anchor for a young club will send a couple of rookies to another team and get an experienced player in return. Sometimes a player seems to fit better in one ball park than another, and so he is wanted by the team that plays in that ball park. Sometimes teams trade to "fill holes"—that is, trade to strenghten a player position that is weak all through the organization. There are as many reasons for trading as there are ball-players on the field, but there is one thing about which almost all major league teams agree. "If you can raise 'em up on the farm, it's a lot better—and cheaper—than going shopping for 'em." In other words, it's better to be able to find players in a club's minor league system than to spend money and trade players for them.

In the '50s and early '60s, when the Tigers were struggling near the very bottom of the American League standings, they were criticized a lot for not looking for new, young talent. Newspapers screamed because scouts weren't sending enough new players into the farm system. Worse yet, not enough of those farm team players were turning out to be good enough to play in the major leagues.

Without making a lot of noise about it, led by Rick Ferrell, the Tigers stepped up their scouting operation. Men like Lou D'Annunzio signed young players like Willie Horton to minor league contracts. And, in the summer of 1964, an awful lot of those new minor leaguers arrived in Syracuse, New York, to play for the Chiefs.

In addition to Willie, the Syracuse outfield included both Mickey Stanley and Jim Northrup. Ray Oyler was at shortstop. Ray Oyler couldn't hit the ball, but he was the best fielding short-stop Willie had ever seen.

All four would make it to the regular Tiger squad in the spring of 1965. So would Syracuse pitcher Denny McLain. The same newspapers that had complained about having no farm team players happily welcomed the new players. They even gave them a special name—"The Boys from Syracuse"—after a popular musical comedy. The "boys" who were in Syracuse that year also included infielder Tommy Matchick and pitcher Pat Dobson, both of whom would become part of the great 1968 Tiger team.

Willie had a good year in Syracuse in 1964. He finished the season batting .288 and had twenty-four home runs. They were long home runs, too. People were beginning to expect that a Willie Horton home run would never be a cheap one. His powerful swing and quick wrists sent almost every homer high into the seats.

This time, Willie was determined not to lose momentum over the winter. When winter ball began, he headed for San Juan, Puerto Rico, to play with *Los Indios de Mayaguez,* the Mayaguez Indians.

"And, starting in left field and batting cleanup, Willie Horton!"

ON HIS OWN

1965 should have been a year of promise. A starting assignment with the Detroit Tigers was Willie's for the earning. All he had to do was look good in spring training. He was a father twice, now. A beautiful baby girl, Terri Lynn, had arrived in the middle of the Syracuse season. He was making enough money that his family never need worry about going back to the projects. Mom and Pop were well-fixed. Patricia and the babies were with him in Puerto Rico. He was sure he'd be able to keep himself fit enough to really show Manager Dressen something in the spring. Already, he was on top of his game, leading the Puerto Rican league in home runs.

Everything should have been wonderful in the new year of 1965, and it was—until New Year's Day was a few hours old.

Because it was technically still part of baseball's Christmas break, Willie was staying with Philadelphia outfielder Alex Johnson. Willie and Alex had known each other since Northwestern High School days. In later years, Alex would run into problems because of what people said was his bad attitude, but right now he was a brand-new major leaguer, proud to be playing ball. He and Willie were having a wonderful time sharing stories of success, and that made the new year seem even more promising.

Then the phone rang.

It was a telephone call that would change Willie's whole world. Alex was there. José Pagan (of the San Francisco Giants) and future Hall of Famer Roberto Clemente were on hand, too. It took all three of them to help tell Willie the news.

Mom and Pop and Willie's brother Billy had been riding in a car driven by one of Billy's friends. There were seven people in the car—all of them laughing and talking and looking forward to a bright new year. It was snowing hard, but, after all, it was winter in Michigan. Mom and Pop took the snow for granted. It was hard for the driver, though. He couldn't see much in front of the car, and less to either side of him. The car headed down the I-94 freeway, not far from Albion, Michigan, when suddenly, there, right in front of it, was an enormous salt truck. The truck was barely crawling along, and it was as wide and solid as a brick wall. Billy's friend hit the brakes. He tried hard to stop, but he couldn't—not in time. The car slammed hard into the back of the truck.

Billy was hurt, but he'd be okay. Pop was dead—killed the moment the car and truck collided. Mom had made it as far as the hospital, but nobody expected her to live.

Willie needed to get back to Michigan as soon as possible, but there weren't any airline tickets to be had—not on New Year's Day. Word was passed frantically. Could anybody help? Lou D'Annunzio was there for support. Along with everyone else, he asked around, seeking a ticket—any sort of ticket. Finally, a baseball official was found who was flying back to New York, and he gave up his ticket to Willie. Willie was assured he would be able to find a flight from New York to Detroit.

Gates Brown, big and solid and comforting, was there to meet Willie's plane when it finally arrived at Willow Run airport, outside of Detroit. "He's pretty shook up," Gater told reporters.

Mom died just thirty-six hours after the accident. Willie got the news in a phone call that came just as he walked into the house.

Willie was numb. He didn't know what to say or do, except for the ordinary things that have to be done when someone dies. He was religious. He believed in God. He had felt close to God ever since the day when he and Munsey walked the railroad track to Appalachia, Virginia. But religion seemed as far away as everything else. Nothing was real.

Jim Campbell and Charlie Dressen telephoned—both on the line at the same time. "If you want to sit out this season, you can," they told Willie. "You're young. You've got a lot on your mind—a lot to do. Baseball can wait for you if you need it to."

It was a generous offer from kind men, but when he heard it,

WILLIE AND THE GATER. The friendship that Willie and the Gater (Gates Brown) formed during Willie's early minor league days would last for a lifetime. Here, dressed in "sweats"—in a picture that dates from the 1970s—they catch their breaths after an off-day workout. (Reprinted with permission from the *Detroit News*.)

Willie knew what he had to do was almost the opposite thing. He was going to make 1965 the greatest season he'd ever had. The season would belong to Pop and to Mom. He'd dedicate it to them both.

Somehow he got through the next few weeks, doing everything that had to be done. Jim Campbell was there at the house part of each day, making sure that Willie knew he wasn't alone.

81

Charlie Dressen and all Willie's baseball friends sent words of encouragement.

This time when he reported to spring training, Willie was in good shape—only a very few pounds overweight. He went to work—hard. Dressen was pleased, and he was proud, too. He knew what kind of strength it took for Willie to play his father's favorite game only a few months after Pop had died.

Then fate gave Willie yet another reason to need that strength. In the spring of 1965, Charlie Dressen had a massive heart attack. Bob Swift, who had managed Willie in Mayaguez, took over the club. As far as anybody knew, Dressen would be back to manage again before the season was over. In fact, by June he was calling the shots, as feisty and impish as ever. But in spring training, Willie felt as if the whole world was rocking underneath him.

Swift platooned Willie in left field with another of the boys from Syracuse—Jim Northrup. Willie faced only left-handed pitchers. Jim was in the lineup against right-handers. Jim wasn't very happy about the arrangement because, even though most left-handed batters can't handle left-handed pitching, Jim's minor league record had been just the opposite. He did as well or better against left handers as he did righties.

Swift stuck to his plan anyway, and, as a result, Willie's batting average and home run total began to climb. By the end of May, he was the starter in left field—for every game. Don Demeter was in center, and Al Kaline was in right.

In June, Charlie Dressen was back and talking about Roy Campanella again. So were the newspapers. Willie knew about Campanella, but he had never met him. Almost on a whim, he decided he'd try to telephone him.

"Campy," as he was called by just about everyone, was no longer playing ball—for the Dodgers or anybody else. He'd been paralyzed in a traffic accident, and now he spent his days working and making public appearances from a wheelchair. Willie's phone call found him in his office. The two men talked for over three hours. Eager reporters asked Willie what they'd talked about. What had he learned? "He just told me to keep on swinging," Willie grinned.

By midsummer, Willie's bat was feared all around the league. He was the talk of the town wherever the day's game was played. Opposing teams hated to see him come to the plate. One morning, after Willie had almost single-handedly won a game against the Boston Red Sox, center fielder Don Demeter joked with his teammates. "Who's guarding Willie tonight?" he laughed. "I'll take first watch!"

The 1965 season, Mom and Pop's season, finished with Willie hitting a decent, if not star quality, .273. More important, he had twenty-nine home runs and 104 R.B.I.'s. This last number made him one of the five top run-producers in the entire American League.

NEW DIRECTIONS

Baseball had always been a part of Willie's life, but in 1965, more and more, it *was* his life. There was so much to do—so much to learn between the foul lines. Just playing baseball, thinking baseball, and talking baseball helped to fill the gap left when Mom and Pop died. There was nothing wrong with that. In fact, Pop would have loved knowing how important Willie was becoming to the Tigers and how important baseball was to Willie.

The trouble was that Willie was turning to baseball at a time Patricia thought he should turn to her. After all, she missed Mom and Pop, too—and she had the children to raise, besides. She didn't exactly resent the game. For several years she had kept close track of Willie's accomplishments when he hadn't had time to do it himself. Willie put the situation this way when he was questioned about it: "We both looked to each other for support, me for the loss of my parents and her for her own career and child raising, and we just couldn't give each other what we needed."

Other couples might have gotten divorced right away. Patricia and Willie were friendly and stayed together "officially," but they began to go their separate ways. After a number of years, they would divorce. For now each worked at getting used to the fact that their marriage was one more thing in their lives that had changed and wouldn't ever change back to the way it had been.

Willie didn't have any trouble keeping busy when games were over, whether or not he had home and family to worry about. His success with the Tigers had made him into a celebrity in Detroit. People asked him to do things, go places, and lend his name to different things that were going on.

It wasn't long before Willie found that what he liked best about his fame was being able to use it to help other people. He spent many, many days just walking around the projects, looking at his old neighborhood, watching it get bleaker and bleaker.

CHARLIE DRESSEN. Both as a player and a manager, Charlie Dressen was known for being "feisty." His energy and drive are obvious in this picture. What does not show is the tremendous care and concern he had for the young players he managed—especially Willie Horton. (Courtesy of the Burton Historical Collection, Detroit Public Library.)

Every time he ran into boys and young men who lived there, he stopped to talk with them. There was always the hope they might see him as an example of what they, too, could do if they had dreams—and worked to make them come true. It was the beginning of a mission that, after baseball, would become the center of Willie's life.

During the winter after the 1965 season, Willie and Phillies pitcher Fergie Jenkins both said "yes" when the Harlem Globetrotters basketball team unexpectedly asked the two baseball stars to take to the road with them during the off-season.

Led by the legendary Meadowlark Lemon, in the mid-1960s the Harlem Globetrotters were in their heyday. Founded in 1927 as a barnstorming club, the Globetrotters quickly became a fixture in the world of basketball. From the beginning, they traveled from town to town (and even country to country) to play. But Willie knew that there was something even more unusual about the Globetrotters. Whether the year was 1935 or 1965 (or 2005, or any other time in the future), to be a Globetrotter meant to be as much a showman as an athlete.

Oh, yes. Then, as now, the Globetrotters came to play basketball—but they did it like no other team in the world. They danced and whirled and passed the basketball between their legs and backward. They used the whole court as a stage. Especially with Meadowlark Lemon on hand, they had enough real basketball talent to win games, but mostly they were all about show. The games were great fun to watch, more fun to play, and the Globetrotters were great guys, but Willie lasted barely one month with them. "I don't know how they handle it," he said later—and he didn't mean the fancy passes.

Instead of playing in a regular basketball league, the Globetrotters played a series of exhibition games against opponents that ranged from college basketball teams to local businessmen and celebrities. Unlike baseball teams that pulled into a town and stayed for several days before moving on, the Globetrotters usually traveled to four or more different towns every single week!

Exhausted, Willie dropped out of the Globetrotters. He had winter ball in Puerto Rico to think about anyway, and spring training wasn't far behind.

FAREWELL, CHARLIE DRESSEN

Now that Willie knew he was a Tiger regular, the days and games were almost predictable—though that didn't mean Willie let up on himself at all. He was always trying to find a way to improve, to do a better job. One day in Baltimore, he asked if he could see Baltimore star Frank Robinson's bat. The veteran outfielder was well on his way toward a lifetime batting average that would be just a few points under .300, and Willie wanted a close look at the tool he was using.

It didn't take Willie long to realize that "Frank Robbie's" bat was a great deal heavier than his own. Willie was using a thirty-two-ounce bat, whippy and light—designed to get around on a ball fast and send it flying out of the ballpark.

Robinson was a solid home run hitter (thirty-three in 1965, and in 1966 he was well on his way to hitting forty-nine), but he used a squat, heavy bat. Willie balanced it in his hand. It must weigh as much as thirty-six ounces. "I'll bet that's it," Willie thought. "I need a heavier bat. I've been swinging too quick."

Charlie Dressen agreed. He urged Willie to try the heavier

bat. Once more, Dressen's advice was right on target. With the
new bat weight, Willie found that it was easier to hit to all fields,
and that likely meant that his batting average would climb. He
still could hit home runs, too. As a matter of fact, his home run
power was increasing. He looked forward to each game and to
each new chance to hit. Charlie Dressen's star pupil was getting
better and better. . . . And then, once again, Willie's world came
crashing down.

Charlie Dressen had yet another massive heart attack.
Everybody was stunned, but a routine had been established the
last time Dressen was hospitalized. Once again Bob Swift took
over management of the club, but this time things did not go as
well. Swift himself fell seriously ill, and third-base coach Frank
Skaff was pressed into management.

Worried about both managers, Willie somehow kept plugging
along. His batting average was down, and his home run total that
year would be only twenty-seven, but he did the best he could—
for himself and especially for Charlie Dressen. Willie had a lot of
ailments of his own to worry about, too. In that one season, he
had a sore knee, a sore foot, a bad hand, and he spent the whole
summer battling a sinus infection. Yet, in spite of that, he hit a
"hot streak" in midsummer, tearing up the league with his hitting. He batted .350 in June; .310 in July.

"If Willie gets healthy, we're all in trouble," joked Acting
Manager Frank Skaff.

Then, while he was still in the hospital, Dressen suffered yet
another heart attack. This attack, coming so soon after the other,
was too much for a sixty-eight-year-old man to survive. On
August 10, 1966, Willie got the news: Charlie Dressen was dead.

All the Tigers were upset. Everybody liked and respected
Charlie Dressen, though none had been as close to him as Willie
had been. Dressen had solid baseball knowledge and a warm heart
to go with his peppery temper. His ball club was just beginning to
"gel." But now he would never come back to lead it to the World
Series he'd promised. Folks shook their heads grimly. Charlie
Dressen would be very much missed by everyone who had anything to do with the Tigers.

Willie sobbed out loud. In less than two years' time, he'd lost
two fathers—Pop and Charlie Dressen. "I want to wear that man's

number," Willie begged, "and do . . . things for him on the field. He's the one who did everything for me." At the time, it seemed like the best way—the only way—to mourn and say goodbye.

Charlie Dressen's uniform number was 7. Single-digit numbers usually go to a club's very top players. Willie's number 23 came closer to matching his newness with the Tigers. Nobody thought Willie would be given number 7, but nobody argued with what Willie said. Everyone knew just exactly how he felt.

⚾⚾⚾ **9** ⚾⚾⚾
Designated Healer

THE COLOR BARRIER

In Stonega, Virginia, when the boys, black or white, finished playing baseball, they'd go find something else to do—fish, or explore, or just hang out together. In Lakeland, Florida, anybody who could play baseball—whether he was black, or white (or green, for that matter)—went to the same field to play the game. But once the players left the baseball diamond, it was all too obvious to Willie that the state of Florida was part of the Deep South, where segregation was far more a fact of life than it ever had been in the mountains of Virginia.

As a boy and as a young man, Willie himself never spent much time thinking about the difference between black and white. Pop and Mom had taught him that the only thing that mattered was how a man felt in his heart. Skin color didn't have a thing to do with whether or not a man was good, or smart, or mean, or dumb. In Stonega it was always a good idea to be careful, but friends were friends. It didn't matter what color they were. In Appalachia Willie had been the only black boy on an all-white team in an all-white league—but he was there because he could play baseball, not because there was some kind of crusade going on.

Willie had close friends who were black. He had close friends who were white. When he played for Duluth, in Minnesota, although black players were segregated from white players (at least in terms of sleeping accommodations), it wasn't a major issue. If six guys had to room together on the road because they were the only black guys on the team, it just meant they could have the darnedest six-way pillow fight you ever saw! Segregation

89

was there and it wasn't right, but nobody made a big deal out of it.

In Lakeland it was a big deal.

Willie found out how big a deal it was the first day he arrived in camp. Right away, he spotted a guy he knew—another rookie. This was great! The two young men were tickled to see each other. "Maybe we can room together!" said Willie's friend. But that wasn't going to happen. The other rookie was white, and whites couldn't room with blacks—not in Lakeland in 1962.

Later on, Willie, staying in a "black" hotel at the other end of town, tried to catch a cab to Henley Field and Tigertown. The first time a cabbie turned him down, he thought his teammates were playing a joke on him. All too soon he realized that white cab drivers all over the South felt quite comfortable turning down black fares. Sometimes the cabbies did it even though they themselves really didn't mind what color the fare was. They were afraid their white riders would refuse to sit in a taxi that had carried black people. The Tigers provided a bus for players who didn't have cars, but if somebody missed the team bus, he had to get to wherever he was supposed to be as best he could. As a result, there were a lot of days when Willie walked six miles to get to Tigertown. "After all," he thought ruefully, "it's the same distance that it took to get from Stonega to Appalachia!"

The Tigers themselves were slow to integrate their team. Although the Dodgers' great Jackie Robinson had become the first African American player in the major leagues back in 1947, it took eleven more years before the Tigers added Ozzie Virgil to their roster. Ozzie was a Dominican, too—not as "black" as many other African Americans. And Ozzie didn't come along until 1958, just three short years before Willie became part of the organization.

But by 1963 and 1964 there were a number of black players on the Tiger squad, and the housing situation was getting ridiculous. Outfielder Billy Bruton led Willie and Gates Brown and their other black teammates to demand that an integrated hotel be built near the Tiger camp. Willie said later that he learned a lot from Billy during those times. Billy showed him how to get results with dignity—without having to make a big protest or demonstration. The hotel was successful—not because of integration, and not "in spite of" integration, either. As Willie hoped, it simply served all the players and all the fans who wanted to be its guests and, as a result, did good business. Willie was proud to have been part of the movement that put it there.

Where the rest of Lakeland was concerned, Willie found he

THE HORTON FAMILY. Willie couldn't have been prouder of his young family. Here, wife Patricia watches as Willie tries to keep a grip on a squirming bundle of energy named Terri Lynn. Darryl is content to sit still—at least for the moment. (Reprinted with permission from the *Detroit News*.)

could eat or shop—that is to say, he could spend money—almost any place he wanted. But living in Lakeland was something else again. There were only a few areas in the community where blacks were allowed to buy homes, and they weren't very nice areas—certainly not places where Willie wanted to raise his children. Eventually he and Pat bought a house in Plant City, a twenty-minute drive from Lakeland. The experience of looking for a house was disappointing. Too many people just didn't seem to care how unfair things were.

In the South, the '50s and '60s were years filled with demonstrations, sit-ins, "freedom rides"—all sorts of attempts made by people who did care and who wanted to convince the rest of the world that segregation of any kind was wrong. Sometimes their demonstrations were so violent that military troops were brought in to maintain order. Schools were integrated under armed guard. The famous artist, Norman Rockwell, painted a picture of a little African American girl all dressed up in her best school clothes and walking into a school. In the picture, you can't see the faces of the grownups who are walking with her. You can see only what the little girl could see—the uniformed pant legs of the army troopers who protect her as she walks into a previously all-white school.

As long as there was something that could be done to help people get along, Willie was just the man to do it. As time went on, he made close friends in Lakeland. Some were especially close. A man named Dennis Gordon became an extra grandfather for Terri and Darryl. Charles and Madeline Brooks were practically family. With these people and others, Willie went to work with a purpose to make a difference in Lakeland. With the support of the National Association for the Advancement of Colored People (the N.A.A.C.P.), Willie and his friends marched and talked and marched some more. Before they were through, Lakeland was a fully integrated city, and Willie had left a large part of his heart in the town that he helped make into a happier place.

In the North, race relations seemed better—at least on the surface. But the problems were still there. Things were segregated more or less according to where people lived, though not by law. Most African Americans lived in large cities, where they had come to work in factories during World War II. Cities tended to be poorer than their surrounding suburbs, so many black children didn't have schools as good as those of their white neighbors. Employers paid higher wages to white employees than to black employees. It was hard for even educated African Americans to be considered seriously for many well-paying jobs. There were exceptions, of course. People like Damon Keith proved that. Still, in the cities, things were about ready to boil over. In Detroit, in the summer of 1967, they did.

In 1967 the Tigers were in the middle of a pennant race. The club that Bob Scheffing had begun to build and that Charlie

Dressen had trained now was one of the strongest in the American League. The new manager, Mayo Smith, was quick to name Willie, still wearing number 23, as his starting left fielder. (Although he had been offered number 7 at the beginning of the season, after he thought about it a while, Willie changed his mind. He would stay with the number that had been his during the days he had played for Dressen.)

The Tigers carried five outfielders that year: Al Kaline, Gates Brown, and the boys from Syracuse—Willie, Jim Northrup, and Mickey Stanley. As it turned out, they needed all five. In the early months of the season, Willie missed a lot of games. He had a series of injuries: a bone spur in his left heel, a sore ankle, a pulled leg muscle. Close to the end of spring training, he collapsed as he ran out a hit to first base. He was carried off the field on a stretcher, past the worried faces of his teammates. "That [the amount of worry] shows you what the players think of Willie," said coach Wally Moses.

Willie's injuries may have happened because, once again, he arrived at spring training more or less out of shape. His extra weight got in the way in a squad game at shiny new Marchant Stadium (built to replace aging Henley Field). Willie lashed a low line drive that got past the center fielder. It turned out to be an inside-the-park home run, and Willie was really puffing by the time he got to home plate. "They made the base paths longer this year," one of his teammates laughed. "Either that, Willie, or your legs are shorter," cracked Jim Northrup.

Willie struggled with more injuries all through the summer, and near the end of the season he had a head cold—one that just wouldn't go away. The "bug" had gone through the entire clubhouse, but Willie couldn't shake it. He missed an entire road trip because he was sick in bed.

And in the middle of that summer, there came the riots.

Willie and his teammates said little publicly about the situation in Detroit. But there was no avoiding it or the damage it had done to the city. Willie kept on working with young people as much as he could. His baseball injuries didn't prevent that. He was absolutely sure that, if young people of all races had hope—that is, if he could give them something to dream about—just knowing that the dream was possible would help them get along in the world. They wouldn't feel as "trapped" by poverty, and by not feeling trapped, they would have taken a first step toward fulfilling the dream. If there were a way for troubled teenagers of both races to hope for something *together,* it would be even better.

"The world doesn't owe you anything," he told every young-ster he saw. "If you have a dream, you need to work hard to achieve it. But don't be afraid to trust other people. You need the support and help of good friends, along with your own efforts, to accomplish your goals in life." Every time he spoke, he thought of the men who had helped him: Ron Thompson, Sam Bishop, Damon Keith—and, of course, Charlie Dressen, and now, more and more, Dressen's boss, Tiger General Manager Jim Campbell.

1967 ended with that heartbreaking loss to the Boston Red Sox (see chapter 1). Would the Tigers have made it all the way to the World Series that year if Willie had been healthy for the entire season? He'd finished the year with just nineteen home runs and sixty-seven R.B.I.'s, though he had hit .274. The last time his average had been close to that number, he'd logged up twenty-nine home runs and 104 R.B.I.'s. Having Willie around all the time certainly could have made a difference. That was part of the reason that every single Tiger, in October of 1967, was pretty darned sure where the team would be in October of 1968. "Next year," they said to each other. "Next year we go all the way."

DESIGNATED HEALER

Every man who was on the 1968 Detroit Tiger squad went on record saying that the team began that season knowing they could win it all.

Willie had made his own special preparations for the year. Over the winter, he had surgery on the leg that gave him the most problems. The soreness didn't go away altogether, but the leg felt more stable. As far as Willie was concerned, a little pain—by itself—was okay. As long as doing so wouldn't cause permanent damage, you just played through it. "Back at Northwestern High School," Willie said to people who worried, "Coach Sam Bishop told us over and over again that 'in your position—and if you want to better yourself—you had better take injuries and pain in stride and go right on playing without complaining.'" Those were words to live by, and Willie kept right on playing.

In 1968 Willie hit thirty-six home runs—more than double his production in 1967. He upped his batting average to .285, partly because he was running faster. His heel was better, and with a special shoe lift in place to protect it, he fairly flew around

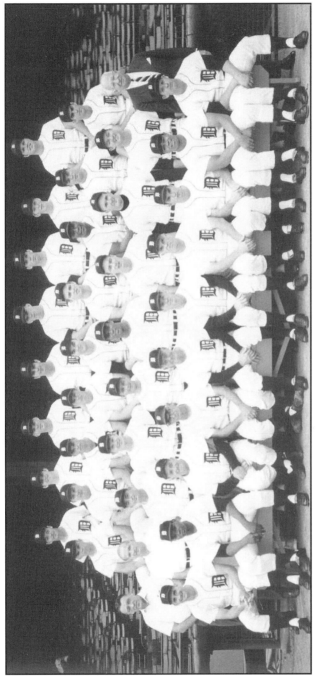

THE 1968 DETROIT TIGERS. This is one of a series of photos taken when the team was choosing its official portrait. *Front row:* Don Wert, John Wyatt, Tony Cuccinello (coach), Wally Moses (coach), Mayo Smith (manager), Hal Naragon (coach), Johnny Sain (coach), Wayne Comer, Willie Horton, Mickey Lolich. *Second row:* John Hand (equipment manager), Bill Behm (trainer), Julio Moreno (batting practice pitcher), Jim Northrup, Ray Oyler, Earl Wilson, Fred Lasher, Don McMahon, Al Kaline, Charlie Creedon (traveling secretary). *Third row:* Dick Tracewski, Norm Cash, Eddie Mathews, Jim Price, Jon Warden, Denny McLain, Gates Brown, John Hiller, Dick McAuliffe. *Fourth row:* Roy Face, Bob Christian, Mickey Stanley, Joe Sparma, Darryl Patterson, Pat Dobson, Tommy Matchick, Bill Freehan. (Courtesy of the Walter P. Reuther Library, Wayne State University.)

the base paths. His hits and home runs came at the right time, too, winning game after game for his teammates.

The team itself had never felt closer. The boys from Syracuse had played together winter and summer for years, and Bill Freehan was a buddy from as long ago as sandlot days. Two springs earlier, Willie looked around the field in Florida and remarked to a reporter, "everybody [here] looks like they love each other." Now he repeated the statement to the same reporter: "That's the reason we're in first place. This team is all friends. . . . We play like a family."

And the Tigers were in first place. From the very outset, it was a season where big things happened—whether it was shortstop Dick McAuliffe's brawl with Chicago pitcher Tommy John or Denny McLain's thirtieth victory, everything that year was larger than life. As the season went on, little by little, all across a city that was still picking up the pieces from last year's riots, radios were turned up louder. By June, if there was a ball game on, Detroiters could walk down the street and not miss an out. Everybody listened to the games. If a game was on television, everybody watched. Appliance stores put TV sets in their front windows and tuned them to the game, sure that they would attract a crowd of potential customers. Teachers in schools citywide and statewide turned a blind eye to narrow cords and hearing-aid-sized earphones. They didn't turn a deaf ear to the hand-held transistor radios, though. They paused in their lectures to be sure everyone in the class could pick up the scores.

In offices, the workers who didn't go down to join the shirt-sleeve crowds at Michigan and Trumbull propped radios against the windows where the reception was best. In the streets, passersby caught the sound and paused to catch the next play. Car radios were on, too, and when the Tigers scored, horns honked and drivers waved at each other.

The vocabulary of baseball, the special words people use to describe things on the playing field, took over the town.

"How many hits did Sparma allow today?" asked an elegantly dressed lady, as she straightened her pillbox hat and pulled on her gloves.

"I see where Mayo's got Willie batting fifth." This time the voice belonged to an old African American man in blue jeans. He was busy sweeping the streets, and he directed his comment to the people crossing with the light.

"Yeah. D'ya think Freehan can handle cleanup, though?" A

WILLIE AND FRIEND. Throughout the 1968 pennant season, Willie stayed close to his young fans. Howell (Michigan) resident Nancy Standler was just six years old when she went all the way to Cobo Hall in Detroit to pose with her hero. Willie, always ready to do anything to reach out to everyone, was at Cobo for a team promotion. (Photo courtesy of Nancy Standler-Brown.)

young advertising executive in suit and tie answered the sweeper.

"I really love Mickey Stanley," gushed a pretty girl at Sanders soda counter. "He's just wonderful."

"Really!" Her friend patted her beehive hairdo and frowned into the mirror on her compact. "He gets a better jump on the ball than anybody, and he certainly can climb that outfield wall!"

Across the street from Hudson's department store, an elderly black gentleman spoke seriously to his grandson. "You want to learn something about playing baseball, you watch Kaline and McAuliffe. Look at the way they behave out on that field. It's easy for Al, and hard for Mac, but they both bear down all the way."

"Hey, ya see where Wilson won his own game with his bat last night?" "'Denny McLain / Denny McLain / There never was any like Denny McLain. . . . '" "How many games are we ahead in the lost column?" "Didja see where Mayo let Willie manage the other night? They won, too!"

It was like that all over town. Never before or since had the city of Detroit been so wrapped up in baseball. The same people who had looked at each other with fear and mistrust—and even hatred—the preceding summer now clustered around portable television sets and cheered on their heroes. Policemen reported that the same boys who loitered on street corners looking for trouble were hanging around the same street corners—but now they were listening to the radio. The elderly black man telling his grandson to keep an eye on Al Kaline's style wasn't talking about some white guy somewhere—he was talking about the man who had patrolled right field in Tiger Stadium for the last thirteen years. Color didn't have a thing to do with it. The fellow bragging about pitcher Earl Wilson's ability to hit wasn't thinking of Earl as a black man, but as someone who had won twenty-two games in 1967 and was on his way to posting a 2.85 E.R.A. in 1968.

It even spilled over into advertising. Plymouth "Roadrunner" cars were sold under Warner Brothers Roadrunner cartoons reading "Beep-beep it to 'em Tigers!" National Bank of Detroit's advertising record, "Go Get 'em, Tigers!" sold like a rock 'n' roll hit. The TV listings in the papers looked like ordinary TV listings, until you looked at them closely:

1:45—Ch.2, Ch. 4 '68 World Series (C). Detroit Tigers Vs. St. Louis Cardinals. Sock it to 'em.

And nobody represented the way the Tigers had brought the city back together any more than Willie Horton did.

THE HEADLINES SAY It All. In Detroit and throughout Michigan, when the Tigers won the 1968 series the celebration was statewide. This edition of the *Detroit Free Press*, with its special handwritten greeting to Tiger fans, was delivered to author Karen Elizabeth Bush. (Photo by K. E. Bush.)

Early in the 1968 season, Willie began thinking of ways to avoid the kind of things that had happened to Detroit in 1967. "One summer of riots was too much," he told people. "I came from the gutter area, and I guess I could forget about it now that I'm a ballplayer. But I can't. The problem is too serious to run away from."

Willie took his ideas right to the top. With the help of Dr. Russell Wright, the Tigers' team physician, he asked to meet with Vice President of the United States Hubert Humphrey. He had plenty to talk about.

Willie had helped form the Northwestern High School Men's Club early that year. The club's purpose was to discuss problems in the city and try to raise money for neighborhood programs.

WORLD SERIES RING. Each person participating on a World Championship team, including some of the people in the team's front office (business office), receives a specially designed ring to commemorate that year's World Series. Backup catcher Jim Price models the 1968 Tigers Championship ring for the camera. (Courtesy of the Walter P. Reuther Library, Wayne State University.)

Along with Willie, club members included outfielder Alex Johnson (then with the Cincinnati Reds), professional football's Henry Carr, and heavyweight boxer Chuck Norris. All had been Northwestern students; all had played for Coach Sam Bishop. Now they wanted to use some of the things Bishop had taught them about good citizenship to help the city.

Willie was absolutely certain that Detroit's problems came from a lack of communication. Black people and white people needed to talk together to solve their problems. He believed the only way to make this happen was to start with young people and get them to share the same ideas and goals. If young people had something to believe in, and had hope, Willie felt they wouldn't want to hurt each other. That was the message he wanted to get across to Vice President Humphrey.

Willie talked about "starting with the kids" every chance he got. He couldn't resist making appearances—usually for free—wherever he thought it would "do the kids some good." The Tiger director of special events, Vince Desmond, set up speaking engagements for Willie—and told people that Willie was a very good speaker. As a matter of fact, Desmond was a little surprised at how well Willie handled audiences. Often ballplayers didn't do

TIGER STADIUM AND THE DETROIT SKYLINE, 1968. The empty ballpark stands guard over the city the Tigers and Willie helped to heal. (Courtesy of the Walter P. Reuther Library, Wayne State University.)

very well when they spoke in public, but Willie had a message to deliver, and he did his best to make people understand.

"You are going to get hurt many times before you grow up," he told schoolchildren and teenagers across Detroit. But it wasn't a message of bitterness. Accepting that life could be tough was just the starting point for young people. It was how they handled that fact that mattered. "Get off the streets," Willie told them. "Keep out of trouble. Keep busy. Play baseball, basketball, football, or any sport you like, but you've got to keep out of trouble."

⚾⚾⚾⚾⚾

Willie gave everything he could to young people when he was off the field. When he was on the field, he gave his team 200 percent. In an article that tried to measure how important each player would be during the World Series, the *Detroit Free Press* looked at Willie's record and wrote:

101

Willie Horton, 26, is the most powerful man playing in the Series. [Willie is] a home run possibility anywhere, anytime, and the man who has given Detroit the big long ball all year. In many ways [he is] the key to the Detroit attack.

Willie was able to stay healthy during most of the 1968 season. He was there to knock in the winning run when Denny McLain won his thirtieth game. (McLain was the first major league pitcher to win that many games since Dizzy Dean had done it in 1934). He was there to make the play of his life and turn the World Series around for the Tigers. But most of all, he was there for all fans, black and white, to cheer and to love.

Baseball didn't have a designated hitter rule in 1968. Pitchers were part of the game and batted for themselves. But if baseball ever had a "designated healer," it was Willie Horton—who helped his ball club bring healing to an entire city.

⚾⚾⚾ **10** ⚾⚾⚾

Willie the Wonder

A Fixture in Left Field

Baseball people refer to a man who plays a position day in and day out for a club as a "fixture." After the 1968 World Series, and right up until he was traded in 1977, Willie and left field in Tiger Stadium were "almost synonymous." (That's another baseball expression—one meaning that he was there all the time.) Willie was a fixture in left field.

This wasn't literally true, of course. Willie's career was filled with injuries, and he missed a good many games. But for the most part, when a fan looked into left field in Tiger Stadium, he (or she) expected to see Willie there. Certainly the fans felt that way after 1968.

However, there was a stretch early in 1969 when Willie wasn't in left field at all. In May of that year he was suspended for failing to go on a road trip with the club. The papers talked about the fact that Willie was being booed because of his injuries—and booing was something he hadn't yet learned to handle. The papers were partly right. Being booed in the home park was tough to take—especially when he wasn't any happier about the injuries than the fans were. But Willie had a more important reason for missing games. He had concerns that went along with the racial issues that were being discussed all over the country. He used his time off to meet with club officials and talk about the need to give young African American ballplayers a better chance with the scouts—and the need to have more African American players on the team.

General Manager Jim Campbell listened and considered what Willie had to say, but he was firm. He expected Willie to "play

103

over" any personal concerns. Willie was welcome back whenever he decided to join the club, but until then he was suspended indefinitely. Suspension meant that he'd receive no pay for any day he was absent. Every game he missed would cost him $340. In 1969, most people needed to work two or three weeks to earn that much money.

The story that went out to the papers had to do with all the booing, not with any racial issues, and that was fine with Willie. He'd learned long ago from Billy Bruton—and others—that often the best results came from honest discussion, not from fancy demonstrations.

In 1968, Willie was known for his hitting. In 1969, he proved to fans and Tiger management that he had developed into a steady and capable outfielder. He didn't do this just by playing good ball—although he did, every time he came to the park. He made his mark as a fielder a little more spectacularly than that.

In one memorable game in Cleveland, it seemed as though everything was being hit his way. When the game was over, Willie had tied a seventy-one-year-old record for a left-fielder, making eleven putouts in eleven chances. Each of the eleven times he'd been given an opportunity to make a play, he'd caught the ball. Each time he caught the ball, he caught it on the fly, meaning the batter was out. In a nine-inning ball game, there are only twenty-seven outs a side. With eleven fly-ball putouts, Willie, all by himself, had accounted for almost half of the Cleveland outs! The *Tiger Yearbook* the following spring was gleeful:

> His bat and his glove both made headlines for Willie Horton in 1969, when he led the Tigers in home runs with 28 and RBIs with 91. He poled three grand slam homers . . . and his fielding caused a sensation in July when he tied a major league record by handling 11 chances with 11 putouts in a game at Cleveland.

Willie was truly a wonder!

Another on-the-field achievement that year earned Willie praise from all kinds of people—but it was one that Willie wished hadn't been necessary.

No matter how much they practice calling for the ball on a play—no matter how alert they try to be—outfielders occasionally get in each other's way. The biggest problem is that this tends to happen when they're running full tilt.

Al Kaline and Jim Northrup went out on the same fly ball.

BAT DAY AT TIGER STADIUM. Young fans reach over the railing so their favorite left-fielder can sign their new bats. (Reprinted with permission from the *Detroit News*.)

Concentrating on the play, they didn't see each other in time, and Northrup ran hard into Kaline. They both went down, and Al didn't get up.

When an accident like that happens, all the players know that it can be serious. The umpires called time, and the Tigers ran toward right field. Of the players on the field, Willie, starting out from his position in left, had the longest run to get there. Bill Behm, Tiger trainer and expert in first aid, had to come all the way from the dugout. Behm had a clubfoot, and he couldn't run very fast. But even if the trainer had been riding a bicycle, Willie saw that he wasn't going to get there in time.

Al had been hit so hard in the collision he had swallowed his tongue. He was unconscious, and, with his tongue blocking his throat, he couldn't breathe. His face was already turning blue from lack of oxygen.

Willie didn't have time to think. He felt as if a tape of his boxing days were playing through his head. Al looked like a boxer who had swallowed his mouthpiece. Over and over, boxing coaches had lectured Willie and his friends about using mouthpieces properly so they wouldn't be swallowed. If you swallowed your mouthpiece and it blocked your airway, you were as good as dead.

Al's airway was blocked. He wasn't breathing—and if you don't breathe, you die. The players clustered around him were trying to open Al's mouth, but his jaws were locked shut.

Willie brushed everybody aside and grabbed Kaline's lower jaw and forced it open. Then he pulled Al's tongue out of the way. "I remembered that when a guy gets knocked out you got to grab him back of the jaw with your fingers and pop it open," Willie explained a few weeks later. "After we got [Al's mouth] open, I got his tongue with my fingers so he couldn't swallow it." Al took a deep breath and then another. Willie kept hold of Al's tongue until he was sure it wouldn't flip backward again.

In the middle of everything, Kaline's jaw clicked shut again, right on Willie's hand. Willie would carry the scar from that bite for the rest of his life, but he didn't mind being bitten at all. It was the rest of *Al's* life he cared about, and now it looked like Al would have a lot more years to live. He was breathing well and his color was coming back. And then, at last, Bill Behm arrived to take over.

Kaline opened his eyes, and the first thing he saw was Willie. Then he saw the manager, Mayo Smith, and Bill Behm. It had all happened so quickly that Al didn't even realize he'd been knocked unconscious. "How'd you guys get out here so fast?" he asked.

Willie got an award for his quick action that day—a different sort of award than he ever would have expected to earn in a baseball game. The Michigan Heart Association made the presentation, and they told Willie that he had very likely saved his teammate's life.

THE SEVENTIES

Willie began 1970 with a shave. During the 1969 season he'd grown a mustache. General Manager Jim Campbell hadn't liked it (the Tigers were expected to be well-dressed and neatly groomed on and off the field), but he hadn't said much about it. Now, with

ALL THOSE BROTHERS AND SISTERS. Willie was a proud Tiger when his picture was included in this collection of photos of most of Clinton and Lillian Horton's children. Willie wasn't the only one of them who was successful in life, but he's easy to spot. He's the only one in a baseball uniform (lower left)! (Photo courtesy of Willie Horton.)

the mustache gone, Campbell was quick to congratulate Willie. "You look a lot younger without it," he said.

"With my pipe in my mouth, I look a lot like you," replied Willie, grinning at the pipe-puffing general manager. He didn't promise to stay clean-shaven, either.

"My daddy wore a mustache," he told everybody, "and Judge Keith wears one. Abraham Lincoln had one. So I guess I'll grow another one this summer."

Willie was in a good mood that season. Right up until the All-Star break (the midpoint in each baseball season), his life had gone better than it had in a long time. He was still grinning at things in general in July when he gave a huge party for the grounds crew (the men who took care of the playing field in Tiger Stadium).

That party was pure Willie. The grounds crew were very important to the Tiger players, but they rarely got much official attention. Willie saw to it that, for one day at least, the groundskeepers would be treated like kings. One of the long-time stadium employees said that it was "the best party we've had since [Tiger Hall of Famer] Hank Greenberg used to invite us out when he was playing."

And then the injuries started up again. Off and on crutches for the rest of the 1970 season, Willie couldn't do much to help his ball club, and his smile began to dim. Over the winter, he worked out and trained, planning to help the Tigers in a big way in 1971.

But two things happened.

First, he and Patricia separated completely. Patricia kept the children at home with her, and Willie moved out of the house. He'd live by himself in Detroit—not too far away, but things felt very strange and final. That was one thing.

The second was that he bought a restaurant. Well, it wasn't exactly a restaurant. But it wasn't a bar, either, even though, when people talked about Willie's troubles, sometimes they blamed it on the "bar business."

Club 23, named for Willie's uniform number, was a social center. It had a place to eat, of course. There was a bar, too, and some meeting rooms. There even was a special room for older people. Sometimes parties would be set up in the club's parking lot, and large groups ate food barbecued outdoors in a wok.

Once Club 23 was established, Willie began to invite area business people to gather there, so they could share in his desire to work with the city's children. Through programs organized at Club 23, eventually as many as 500 children at a time were able to see ball games—for free.

Yet Club 23 did create at least one big problem. Remember all that weight Willie gained just driving through West Virginia?

Now he owned a restaurant.

Maybe it was because of the days he didn't have enough to eat when he was a child. Maybe it was because eating was something that was always good, even when everything else seemed to be going bad. Whatever the reason, Willie just couldn't resist good food. When he came into camp for 1971 spring training, Willie was as far overweight as he had been the year Charlie Dressen gave him the ham. Only this time the manager wasn't Charlie Dressen. It wasn't Mayo Smith, either. In 1970, the Tigers had finished in fourth place—their worst finish in five years. Mayo was gone, and in his place was Billy Martin.

Martin was a work-hard, play-hard kind of man. He liked to party with his players, but he didn't have a lot of patience with them during a game. He took one look at Willie, twenty pounds over his playing weight, and he lost his patience right then.

Willie's season went downhill from there. He still had problems to deal with at home, as well as facing his usual struggle with injuries. Martin didn't particularly care what was going on in Willie's head; he wanted results.

Willie got unhappier and unhappier. He wasn't playing his best. Usually happy-go-lucky—the easiest of the Tigers to get along with and the most fun to be with—now he was sour and sullen. "He's like a bear," worried Jim Campbell. Over and over, Campbell urged Willie to see Judge Damon Keith and talk through whatever was bothering him. The *Michigan Chronicle,* an African American newspaper, even wrote a long editorial scolding Willie for letting his people down—for not being a good role model any more. But none of this did much good. Willie continued to play haphazard, careless ball and to growl at people.

Billy Martin wasn't having a good year, either. There was the "Lakeland thing" to think about. Martin, a white man, got into trouble with the Lakeland police, mostly for suggesting they were racist. To give him credit, Martin, too, was worried about Willie. He knew that no other manager had ever had a problem of any kind with him, and he couldn't figure out why he had so many.

Reporters asked Willie what he thought of Billy Martin. Did he hate him? Willie was quick to say "no!" but he added, "we're not as close as we should be. I don't believe in going around with the manager after the game. He's more to me than a ball player. I respect him too much as a manager."

That was part of the problem. Martin was a lot younger than any manager Willie had ever known, and he liked to go out on the town with his players after the games. It was partly because he liked to "party" and partly because, that way, he got to know his men better. Willie, religious and home-loving, just didn't fit into that kind of life. Martin didn't understand. He thought Willie was sulking.

Late in the season, Willie was hit in the eye by a pitch. The injury was bad enough to put him in the hospital. Once he was released, he couldn't play for a month. The baseball year was nearly over when Martin, without checking to see how Willie was feeling in his first days back in uniform, threw him into a game. It was for Willie's own good, but Willie didn't see it that way.

Almost immediately, Willie failed to run out a play—that is, he didn't run to first base after he'd hit the ball. Billy Martin angrily sat him down on the bench (took him out of the lineup) for the rest of the game. Willie blew up. He left the bench and headed into the clubhouse. Martin fined him $100 and followed him up the tunnel. Willie blew up again, and Martin raised the fine. "That's $200," he said—and then, "that's $300." When he reached "That's $1,000," Willie shut up.

It was an uneasy peace. With all Willie's troubles and injuries, by the end of the season there were rumors of a trade. "Willie for a pitcher?" the papers wondered. "Definitely not," replied Jim Campbell. In spite of everything, Willie's numbers had been decent in 1971—twenty-two home runs, seventy-two R.B.I.'s, and he'd hit .289. He'd be starting in left field during the 1972 season.

Willie started there, but he almost didn't finish there.

Spring training, 1972, began almost where things had left off in 1971. Willie was unhappy. Martin was frustrated.

Finally, Willie was called into Jim Campbell's office. Jim Campbell and Billy Martin were there, puffing away comfortably on their pipes. Frank Skaff, now chief scout for the Tigers, had managed Willie before. He was on hand to help Willie and Billy Martin work out their problems.

But the meeting had hardly begun before it ended. There was time for some casual conversation, and Campbell doubled Willie's current fine—just for starters. Then he began to lay down the law. "Willie," he said, "if there's something bothering you, come to me or go to Billy and sit down quietly and talk to him."

Campbell didn't leave it there, though. There was a larger problem that affected more players than just Willie. He turned to Billy Martin. "You do the same," he said. "If there is something you need to say to Willie—or any player—take him in your office and discuss it *quietly.*"

Suddenly, to everyone's surprise, Martin threw his pipe (a gift from Campbell) across the room and stood up. "You can't tell me how to run a ball club. Just get yourself another manager!" he snapped, and walked out the door.

Martin's walkout only lasted a day. No one was sure why he

'72 DIVISIONAL CHAMPS. The celebration in the clubhouse when the Tigers won the 1972 Eastern Division championship was almost as wild as when they won the 1968 title. Deliriously happy with the victory, Al Kaline and Willie hug each other. Al is soaking wet because someone has poured a bottle of champagne over him. (Reproduced with permission from AP/Wide World Photos.)

had lost his temper—maybe because he felt he had been criticized in front of too many other people. "Billy is Billy," shrugged Jim Campbell. The Tigers won the Eastern Division Championship in 1972, but Willie had the worst year of his life. He batted a lowly .231, hit just eleven home runs, and had only thirty-six R.B.I.'s. He didn't get to play much. Billy Martin was clear about that. There were no more personal problems between the two men, but if Willie wasn't hitting, he wouldn't be playing. This time the trade rumors were serious—but no other team wanted Willie. He represented nothing but injuries and trouble.

Some of Willie's friends thought that Club 23 was causing many of his problems. Certainly there were things involved with running the business that took Willie's mind off the playing field.

Then things began to change. In fact, they'd started to look up a little toward the end of that awful 1972 season. Willie was talking to Damon Keith again, and Keith helped him with a whole lot of issues. At home, things were working out, too. For Willie, the most important thing on the home front was that he and his family—he and his children—be together, and they were. On the road, Willie had new roommates—baseball's six-foot, seven-inch "gentle giant" Frank Howard, now a Tiger, and later, shortstop Eddie Brinkman. The three were inseparable friends. Willie was his happy self again. And of course, from a baseball standpoint, the best thing of all was that the Tigers won the 1972 American League Eastern Division championship.

Willie's numbers began to climb again in 1973. Willie and Billy Martin were getting along—well. Then, in 1974, Martin was gone. There was a new manager, Ralph Houk. "The Major," as he was called, was supposed to be a "people person," but he didn't understand Willie's growing desire to help the younger players on the team. With thirteen years of organized ball behind him, Willie was a veteran. Veteran players often act as unofficial coaches, but Houk didn't see things that way. Willie managed to keep his totals steady in 1974, but he didn't get much playing time. And he didn't get to use his baseball knowledge to help his teammates. Yet the following season things got better—for a while.

The American League now had the "designated hitter" ("D.H.") rule. Under this rule, instead of making the decision whether to pinch-hit for a pitcher each time the pitcher came to bat, a manager could "designate" a pinch hitter to bat for the pitcher all through the game. Under this rule, designated hitters didn't play in the field, and the pitchers never came to bat. The first Tiger designated hitter was Willie's pal Gates Brown, who long had a reputation for being the best pinch hitter in either league. He was followed by Al Kaline. Kaline and others filled the D.H. role in 1974, but Al retired that year. By 1975, the Tigers needed to pick a new designated hitter.

The spot was a natural place to play a man whose injuries kept him off the playing field but who could still hit the ball. Ralph Houk made Willie the Tigers' designated hitter.

Willie wasn't sure how he felt about being a D.H. He wanted to really *play*—in the outfield as well as at bat. But the D.H. position seemed to work out well for him. His batting average dropped a little bit (it had been .316 in '73 and .298 in '74) but as D.H. he had twenty-five home runs and ninety-two R.B.I.'s—the most he'd had in ten years. He came to bat 615 times in 1975. He'd never had that many at-bats before. When the American League checked his totals, he was named Comeback Player of the Year. He began to get offers from other clubs. Teams in Japan, especially, offered good money for a player they considered to be a great American slugger—a man who could hit home run after home run.

Willie stayed "hot" into the beginning of the following season. In May 1976, the league named him Player of the Month. In midsummer, he was Player of the Week (July 28–August 3).

⚾⚾⚾⚾⚾⚾

Willie had been in the major leagues for thirteen years and in baseball for fifteen. Most of those were good years. He felt he could stay with the Tigers forever. At the end of the 1976 season, he set his heart on a multi-year contract—one that would assure that he'd be a Tiger for more than one more season. But by late December there was still no contract. He was still unsigned.

"I've got a feeling something's up," he told a reporter. "I know I could pick up a three-year contract with five or six teams. Several teams have indicated to my agent that they would offer me a heck of a contract.

"I don't want to leave. The Tigers are part of my family. But I've got to think of the future. It'd be different if I was 35 or 36. But I'm not. I'm only 33. And I'm not even asking for a raise. If these other teams can offer that kind of contract, I don't see why the Tigers can't."

In the end, Willie settled for a one-year, $100,000 contract. He went into spring training still eager to use his experience to help the younger players on the club. After all, helping young people, black or white, was what Willie liked to do better than almost anything in the world—except maybe play baseball. If he helped young players, it would be like paying back the older Tigers who had helped him when he was a youngster "coming up."

"[When I was a young man] I listened to my father," Willie explained to a reporter, "and he always said listen to the older guys." Now Willie was going to be the "older guy" that young players would seek out for advice. He figured he'd better get to know the rookie players and understand them before he tried to answer a bunch of questions. To the reporter, he said, "I try to understand their ways because my ways are old. Their ways are much better. It's easier for me to understand their ways than for them to understand my old ways."

Willie talked to the reporter on April 5.

By April 12, just one week later, and with the season under way, Willie's eagerness began to fade. He was spending so much time on the bench that it was hard for him to stay interested in the game. Pregame practice seemed like a waste of time, especially if Ralph Houk wasn't ready to let him work with the younger players the way a veteran normally would do. So Willie sat out a couple of practices. Houk was furious.

"I won't put up with that kind of stuff," he told Willie. "I can't have a ballplayer around who won't do his work. If you don't want to take batting practice and do the other things that are expected of the members of this team, you can take your uniform and go home."

Willie went back to his locker and sat down. He thought that Houk was being bullheaded—and wasting what he, Willie, could do for the club. Still, he promised to take batting practice and do anything else Houk wanted him to do. He never dreamed what Houk's next order would be.

Barely ten minutes later, Houk called Willie back into his office. Houk hadn't known about it when he was chewing Willie out, but Willie wasn't even a Tiger any more. Jim Campbell had traded him to the Texas Rangers!

Willie took the news with mixed emotions. He had the right to reject the trade. He'd played major league ball long enough for that. But he thought about it for a while. He'd been unhappy once the season started because, with young Steve Kemp doing well in left field and Rusty Staub solidly planted in right, he wasn't getting much chance to play ball. He hadn't even D.H.-ed in every game. Willie felt sure Texas wouldn't have spent the money to get him if they planned to have him just sit around. Maybe the trade was the best thing that could have happened to him. He'd have to keep focusing on that—on the good part of the news.

"But," Willie told everybody, "as long as I live, I'll be a part of the Tigers—a part of Detroit."

The day that Willie packed his bags, the only members of the 1968 World Championship team left with the Tigers were relief pitcher John Hiller and Mickey Stanley, the last of the boys from Syracuse.

⚾⚾⚾ **11** ⚾⚾⚾

Mull Digging

THE BADDEST YEAR

D uring the first weeks after he'd been traded to Texas, there were a lot of nights when Willie cried. He'd been a Tiger for so long it was part of who he was. He went through the motions of press interviews. He told people he "felt good about the trade." He was "looking forward to playing regularly. I hope to be some kind of credit to the team. I'm happy they wanted me."

It was the right thing to say, anyway. And there was a lot of truth in it. He found himself remembering his father's voice from back in the old days in Virginia. "You gotta be a mull digger," Pop used to say when things were rough. "We all got to be mull diggers."

Willie was never sure exactly where the term "mull digger" came from. "Mull" is another name for the soil that is deep underground, where earth meets bedrock. When a man hits bedrock, he can't dig any further. So, probably, a mull digger is somebody who works as hard as he possibly can, digs as far as he possibly can go, and doesn't complain about it.

Willie wanted to be a mull digger. At least he wanted to work hard enough to be one. That was as much "who he was" as being a Tiger was "who he was." And to be a mull digger, he felt as if he had to play baseball—really play. It didn't feel right to sit on the bench. He wanted to be out there in the outfield. It was hard to leave Detroit, but if he could play in Texas. . . .

But he couldn't. It turned out that Texas had made the trade just so they would have an extra outfielder to trade to somebody else.

Willie was angry. He made enough noise about it that the Rangers decided he was the first outfielder they'd let go if a trade

117

opportunity came along. The following spring, Willie was traded to the Cleveland Indians.

A funny thing about that trade is that it sent Willie back to Lakeland, Florida, and the Tigers for a couple of days. He wasn't Tiger property, of course, but he went to Lakeland to work out. The Cleveland trade had happened on the day he reported to the Texas spring training camp. He couldn't stay with Texas to start his workouts, and it would take a little while to get his family organized and headed for the Cleveland camp. So he stopped off at Marchant Field in Lakeland!

In Cleveland, it was pretty much the same story. Willie arrived, anxious to play, and things started off well—at first. He tried hard to fit in. He hosted cookouts for his teammates. He helped any of the younger players who wanted help, but, by June, he was a "part-time designated hitter." Being a D.H. instead of an outfielder was bad enough, but part-time?

His manager said it was because he wasn't hitting the ball well. He was batting .356—an outstanding average—on the day the decision was made to make him part-time, so claiming he wasn't "hitting the ball well" didn't make any sense. He even was leading the Indians in R.B.I.'s. Confused and upset, Willie quit hitting—not on purpose, but because he couldn't concentrate. The fans thought he was hurt. Cleveland executives thought he was sulking. Willie didn't know what to think. But, day after day, he wasn't in the lineup. His average dropped to .259, but he still was second in home runs on the ball club. One of the things that hurt the most was that he felt close to the club. It wasn't like being a Tiger, but he cared about the people on the team.

At the end of June, the Indians traded him to Oakland.

Another team meant another beginning. For a guy who wanted to be a mull digger, beginning anything was a good omen. Willie hauled out his old batting helmet—the same one he'd used with the Tigers—and scraped the Cleveland Indian emblem off of it. It would have to be painted again, but somebody found him an Oakland A's letter to glue on the front.

Once again, Willie came to the park to play. Once again he was a pinch hitter. Once again he hit for average, batting .313— trying to be a mull digger. Once again he was traded—this time to Toronto. A sarcastic Oakland newspaper reporter wondered what would have happened if Willie had batted .400. Maybe that would have gotten him sent to the minor leagues! "Such is life," the reporter wrote, "with the A's, who had been searching all season for right-handed power, only to discover it in Horton, then send him packing to Toronto [in a trade] for Rico Carty."

In the course of a single season, Willie had played fifty games with Cleveland and thirty-two games with Oakland—and he would have only thirty-three games in a Toronto Blue Jays uniform.

Willie was in Toronto just long enough for one very unpleasant—and potentially dangerous—thing to happen.

Willie was staying in Toronto with the team, but his family still lived in Detroit. It was a houseful. There were three boys at home now—Albert and Deryl (who belonged to Gloria Reed, a woman Willie had been dating since his separation from Patricia), and Patricia and Willie's boy Darryl. Toronto was close to Detroit, and the boys all wanted to see Willie play at Exhibition Stadium. Along with Gloria, they drove to Toronto to spend the weekend.

Everything was wonderful until the day Gloria and the boys were ready to head back home. They loaded up the car so the family could to go back to Detroit right after the game. Willie had his own car, of course, and he and Gloria headed for the park in it— the boys following behind them in the other car with the luggage. As the two cars pulled up outside the ballpark, Willie looked in his rear-view mirror. There was a tangle of people milling around the boys' car. "What in the world is going on back there?" Willie asked Gloria—and he got out of the car and headed toward the fracas.

The boys had barely stepped outside their car before a small group of men began to harass them. The boys stood their ground, and things got ugly very fast. Mounted policemen, there to oversee the recreational area that included Exhibition Stadium, rode over quickly to bring order. In the process, one of the horses stepped on Deryl. In the few minutes it took for Willie to arrive, everybody began shouting, and it looked as if people might really get hurt. Willie rushed up to see if he could help—ready to do anything he could to calm things down.

One of the mounted policemen saw a man hurrying toward what was looking more and more like a real fight. He didn't recognize Willie as one of the Blue Jays. He just figured Willie was there to cause more trouble. The officer swung his riot stick at Willie's head—hard. Riot sticks are long wooden clubs. They are heavy, about three times as thick as a broomstick, and fastened securely to the wrists of the policemen wielding them. They are designed to be used in crowd control, and this one caught Willie just right, knocking him out. Down he went. He stayed unconscious for several minutes.

119

That settled everything down, all right. An ambulance was called, and everybody went off to the hospital. The boys—Albert, Deryl, and Darryl—were treated for cuts and that stepped-on foot. Darryl's neck hurt. The police decided that everybody had been disturbing the peace, and they charged Willie, Gloria, Albert, and Deryl—but not Darryl. Perhaps they thought that a sore neck was punishment enough. The three Toronto men who had started all the trouble also were charged with causing a disturbance. Nobody seemed to notice that all Willie had done was try to help.

Because Willie had lost consciousness, the doctors told him he'd better not play ball right away. He sat out the following night's game, figuring that the whole episode was a fitting cap to what he often called "the baddest year."

It didn't end there, though. There was less than a month left of the season, and through it all, Willie didn't feel right. The playing field started to look different to him. Things seemed to change from day to day. He couldn't concentrate when he talked to people.

He continued to feel "not quite right" after the season was over. And it got even worse. One day, he thought he was driving to Detroit. To his surprise, he ended up in Cleveland. Finally, he blacked out completely and ended up in a hospital, drifting in and out of a coma. It was four or five months before he felt "normal" again. He was still fighting blackouts the day he left for Venezuela and winter ball.

THE ANCIENT MARINER

Released by the Blue Jays, Willie itched to play real baseball again. His friend Cookie Rojas was managing a club in Valencia, Venezuela, and he persuaded Willie to come there to play. Willie would be playing winter ball again, just as he had done when he was a rookie. Only this time, very quickly, there was a big difference. Rojas wanted Willie to take over as manager. Still under the weather from the accident in Toronto, Willie wasn't sure he could handle the responsibility, but he agreed to try. To his joy, he found that the need to concentrate on the games and focus on his young players helped him recover that much faster.

Under Willie's leadership, the Valencia team won the Caribbean World Series. After 1978, "the baddest year," Valencia felt like paradise. There was a bonus, too. While he was playing,

Willie attracted the attention of scouts who had come to the Caribbean to take a look at the rookies.

Two years before, in 1977, the American League had added again to the total number of its teams, and the Seattle Mariners were born. They were an "expansion team," traditionally the lowest of the low in the standings. In their first two seasons, the Mariners were traditional, all right. They lost almost exactly two-thirds of their ball games. Fans were staying away from the ball-park, and the whole franchise was in danger of folding. The organization desperately needed help, and the scouts saw something in Willie that made them think he could provide it.

At last Willie could be a mull digger! At last somebody really, really needed what he could do for a ball club. Seattle was ready to talk contract. The team made Willie a good offer, one that reflected his experience and track record in baseball. Willie thought about it.

Something had happened while he was playing in Venezuela. Willie called it "finding the little boy in me again." He was learning things—playing baseball in a different way. He felt as eager to play as he had when he was a rookie, and he didn't want to lose the feeling. He asked the Mariners if they'd sign him to a rookie contract—just $36,500, baseball's minimum salary. If they put "incentives" in the contract, he would be paid what he was worth—as long as he played as well as he should. He figured that way he would keep his "edge." He could keep on feeling like a little boy who loved playing and learning the game.

Willie's attitude about D.H.-ing had changed, too. In Venezuela, he discovered that sitting on the bench, watching the game while he waited for his turn at bat, brought with it an unexpected bonus. Studying what was happening all across the playing field had turned him into an excellent manager. Now that he knew he could feel involved in the game while he was on the bench, he would be a more effective designated hitter, too.

In that 1979 season, Willie never missed a ball game. He D.H.-ed in each game, and "hitting" certainly describes what he did. He batted .279, hit twenty-nine home runs, and chalked up 106 R.B.I.'s—the largest R.B.I. total of his entire career. The American League named him both Comeback Player of the Year and Designated Hitter of the Year. Seattle fans adored him. They called him "The Ancient Mariner."

Here was a chance to help more young players, too. Willie called meetings and talked to his teammates when things didn't go well. He taught them how to play with pride. The Mariners still faced a losing season, but the quality of play was better. The spirit on the field extended into the stands. Everybody was having a good time with baseball again.

Over Willie's locker, where his name normally would be, he put a sign. In great big letters, it said "MULL DIGGER." In the Seattle scorebook that year, a two-page article was titled "King of the Mull Diggers." Fans clamored to know how Willie could do so well after having had such terrible seasons in 1977 and 1978. "The only difference is that I'm playing, that's all," he explained. "I wasn't given the opportunity to play in Cleveland. Don't ask me why. I don't know. Nobody ever told me the reason. It was the first time in my life I didn't have a chance to fight for something I wanted, something I knew I could still do. . . . I'm just grateful to my family and the people who never lost faith in me."

Willie could forget any bitterness he still felt about his experience in Cleveland when he looked around him in Seattle. In June, he hit his 300th career home run.

Figure twenty-five men for each team. Then realize that, by the end of the twentieth century, there were twenty-six major league teams. That means that in modern baseball there are approximately 750 players out on the field in any given year. Over time, thousands and thousands of men have played major league ball. In all of baseball's history, only forty-three of those men ever hit 300 home runs in a career. And now Willie was one of them.

The Mariners dedicated a whole game day to Willie. 44,000 fans packed the park.

300 home runs? A "Willie Horton Day"? "Comeback Player of the Year"? 1979 could have been a good place for Willie to stop— a good year to retire. But mull diggers don't quit.

Willie went back to Valencia to manage a second season in winter ball. That time he took his team to second place in their league.

In the spring he returned to Seattle for the 1980 season, expecting to pick up where he'd left off in 1979. But he'd caught an odd skin infection in Venezuela. His hands were sore and raw, and he couldn't grip the bat well. Eventually, his batting average dropped so low that he asked the Mariners not to post it on the scoreboard.

By the time the 1980 season was over, once again Willie was in a situation where he had to fight for a chance to be in the lineup. He needed just seven more hits to reach a total of 2,000

THE ANCIENT MARINER. Willie hit 325 home runs in his career, thirty-seven of them—including number 300—when he was with the Seattle Mariners. Because he was so much older than the rookie players who made up the expansion team, fans called him "the Ancient Mariner," after the character of the same name in Samuel Taylor Coleridge's poem. (Reprinted with permission from the *Detroit News*.)

BUSY WITH THE BEAVERS. In this photograph, taken on a warm day in 1983, Willie pauses to catch his breath between innings. The fierce fellow in the background looks as if he might be a Tiger, but if you look hard, you can see those Portland Beaver teeth! (Courtesy of the Walter P. Reuther Library, Wayne State University.)

career hits. It would have been a nice achievement to go with his 300 home runs, but it wasn't to be.

Learning Not to Play

Willie went on the spring bus tour with the Mariners to promote the team. He talked to fans about the game and all the things the team could expect to do in the 1981 season. When the tour was over, it was almost time for spring training, and Willie felt ready to start again. But the Mariners had a surprise for him. There had been a trade with Texas the preceding year—one of those trades that include "a player to be named later." Willie was that player. They needed Willie to promote the team, but he wouldn't be needed in Seattle as a player. Instead, Willie was a Texas Ranger again.

Still eager to play baseball for anybody who needed him, Willie headed for spring training with the Rangers. He had an outstanding "grapefruit" season—as good a spring as he could remember. He felt ready to take on the whole American League, once the season started.

But it didn't work out that way. The Texas Rangers had a lot of outfielders, and they also had enough depth on the bench that they didn't need another designated hitter. Willie was given his release. He wasn't a Texas Ranger any more. He wasn't anything.

Willie just was too old to be a major leaguer—or at least that's what the major league teams seemed to be telling him.

He couldn't just stop playing baseball altogether. He thought about Japan. To Japanese ball clubs, he still looked like "Willie the Wonder," able to hit the long ball whenever it was needed. But Japan was way, way too far away from his family. Besides, he wanted to stay where major league scouts were more apt to find him.

Portland, Oregon, had a minor league team—the Beavers. It was a Triple-A club, so its quality of play was good. More than that, there were a lot of men on the team that Willie had played against in the major leagues, and some of them were top players. The Beaver's best starting pitcher was none other than Luis Tiant. So Willie tried out with the Beavers—and made the team. He would be a Beaver for two years. Then he played a year in Mexico. But that was it. There were no major league offers, and no other minor league situations that looked interesting. Grudgingly, Willie had to admit that even a mull digger has to quit sometime.

GENE 'N' ROY. When he was a child, Willie's heroes were cowboys. Gene Autry—who takes a moment here to encourage Champion to smile for the camera—was a favorite, but Willie thought that the very best was Roy Rogers—shown with his great golden horse Trigger. By the time Willie was an adult, Gene Autry owned a baseball team (the California Angels) and their paths crossed. Understanding how important cowboy heroes are, even to grown-ups, Autry saw to it that Willie got to meet

Roy Rogers. Rogers wasn't directly involved in baseball, but he was a life-long baseball fan—particularly of the Cincinnati Reds and Los Angeles Dodgers. (Photo of Gene Autry courtesy of the Walter P. Reuther Library, Wayne State University. Photo of Roy Rogers courtesy of the Roy Rogers—Dale Evans Museum.)

Baseball wasn't entirely finished with Willie in 1981. He had a lot more to give to the game, and eventually he would find that it still could "give back" to him. But Willie's playing days were over.

Willie looked back over his seventeen years on the playing field and thought what baseball had brought him. There were the career milestones, of course: from his first major league hit, through the great days with the World Champion Tigers, to Willie Horton Day in Seattle. But baseball was more than just his adventures on the field. There were all the wonderful people who had helped him. There were the fans who cared about him and the kids on the street that he tried so hard to help.

He'd met so many famous people through baseball, too. He'd even got to meet Roy Rogers and Gene Autry! Yes, baseball certainly had been good in unexpected ways. Willie thought for a moment about his old cowboy heroes.

No longer a cowboy star, Gene Autry actually had ended up in baseball. He owned the California Angels baseball team. The Angels, one of the first expansion teams, had come to the American League as the Anaheim Angels in 1969. Eventually the Tigers played against the Angels, and Willie got to meet his old cowboy hero.

Of course, meeting Gene Autry was special, but it couldn't hold a candle to meeting Roy Rogers. Rogers also lived on the West Coast, and during one of the Tiger road trips to California, Willie was asked if he wanted to meet his all-time favorite cowboy star. Rogers wasn't involved in the business of baseball the way Gene Autry was, but he was a serious baseball fan. He was far more than just *willing* to be introduced to Willie Horton. As for Willie? It took him about half a second to say, "You bet!" He even had a chance to see Trigger. The great golden horse had died many years before, but Roy Rogers didn't bury him. Instead, Trigger was sent to a top-notch taxidermist—a man who worked on animals that were put on display in museums. Now, stuffed, Trigger stood on display in Rogers' home.

Willie stared at Trigger for a long time. It was hard to explain to anyone how he felt. His throat ached and his eyes smarted—but it wasn't just from seeing Trigger. He was thinking about a little boy from the projects who never dreamed of the things that would happen to him because of baseball.

ⓄⓄⓄ **12** ⓄⓄⓄ
Now What?

A Sad Business

Playing baseball wasn't the only thing that ended for Willie in 1980. Bad things come in threes, they say.

Event number two was a lot closer to home. He and Patricia had drifted further and further apart over the years, ever since Mom and Pop died. They kept in touch and saw to it that the children were raised correctly, but they weren't really married any more—and they hadn't been for a long time. Divorce was overdue, but when it came, it was—at least for a time—an expensive, unpleasant thing.

That set the stage for problem three: money—Willie's money, and what someone else had done with it.

Willie made a great deal of money playing baseball, but he never really handled it himself. As long as Damon Keith was his agent, that didn't really matter. But then Keith became a federal judge and had to drop other kinds of work. He resigned as Willie's agent, and Willie hired a man named Charles Dye.

In the days when Willie was playing ball, "making a lot of money" didn't mean earning the kind of money that ballplayers in later years would bring home. Willie's fortune consisted of not much over $100,000 a year—and there were many years when he earned far less than that.

Like other ballplayers of the mid-twentieth century, Willie knew he had to have a business career to provide income after he was no longer playing, but he wasn't worried about it. He had the Club 23. It was doing well. He also started a company called the Willie Horton Construction Company.

What Willie didn't know was that Charles Dye had thrown away a lot of money on bad investments, and, worse yet, he hadn't properly prepared Willie's income tax returns.

Just about the time that Willie and Patricia were divorcing, Willie heard from the Internal Revenue Service (I.R.S.). It was not good news. He owed the I.R.S. so much money in back taxes, it didn't look as if there were any way he could pay it off in his lifetime.

To say that Willie was scared is an understatement. But, he figured, if trusting people (that is, Dye) had gotten him into this mess, maybe trusting people could get him out of it, too. He went to see the I.R.S.

This time, Willie's faith in people served him well. The I.R.S. agents weren't ogres at all. They were kind and helpful, and they worked with him. He had to declare bankruptcy and close both his businesses, but he would be able to repay his debts.

When three bad things happen, there should be three good things in return. Getting his financial situation straightened out certainly was one good thing. A second was the way things worked out after his divorce from Patricia.

No one stayed angry. Willie always counted as one of his greatest blessings the fact that his family always stayed together. Once the divorce was settled, he and Patricia could be friends again. And now there was Gloria.

Gloria Reed had gone to Northwestern High School with Willie and Patricia, and she had been a family friend during all the years since then. Now that Willie and Patricia were divorced, Gloria and Willie could be much more serious about each other. It wasn't long before they were married. It was wonderful for Willie, and it was wonderful for the children as well, because they all loved Gloria, too. She was a mother to seven of them—three boys (Albert, Deryl, and Darryl) and four girls (Terri, April, Pam, and Gail). And, because everyone stayed friends, Patricia wasn't ever that far away. Willie's family included two loving mothers, not just one—and all eighteen grandchildren got a whole bunch of hugs from two grandmothers.

After a little work, the third good thing came along, and it was all that Willie needed to feel truly blessed. He might not be playing any more, but he was back in baseball.

Coach Horton

In truth, Willie never had really gone that far away from the game. It just felt that way because he wasn't out there patrolling left field.

Willie was good at managing—no doubt about that. He'd found that out in Venezuela. But he'd also found out that he didn't like managing very much. Coaching was something else. Coaching, with its direct contact with young players, was fun. Maybe he'd learned to feel that way when he played for Charlie Dressen all those years ago. Dressen had loved to spend time with his rookie players. Whatever the reason, there was no question in Willie's mind. Coaching was something he wanted to do.

In '83 and '84, when the Oakland Athletics needed a roving hitting coach—somebody to travel around their minor league system and work with players on all levels—Willie jumped at the chance. A year later, he accepted the same position with the Detroit Tigers.

The Tigers had just won a World Championship—their first since 1968. It was an exciting time to be around the club. It just plain felt right to be a Tiger again. And there was something else, besides. During the 1984 season, Gates Brown had been the major league hitting coach for the Tigers—as good a hitting coach as they'd ever had—but for a number of reasons the Gater didn't expect to be back in 1985. If Willie accepted the minor league assignment, he had a shot at eventually getting Gates's job.

And then, before the 1985 season was very old, Willie got a telephone call from New York.

A month after the season started, owner George Steinbrenner hired Billy Martin to manage the New York Yankees—again. (Martin had a history of being hired and fired by Steinbrenner—most recently in 1979.) Thirteen years had gone by since the time Martin had managed Willie in Detroit. During those thirteen years, Martin had been forced to admit that his aggressive managing style didn't always work with all players—just as it hadn't worked with Willie. Billy Martin had kept an eye on Willie's career during all that time, too, and he knew about Willie's reputation for being able to work with young people.

Now Martin needed to hire a coach who understood what "Billy-ball" was all about—preferably somebody who had played for or with him and understood his approach to the game. And that same coach had to be somebody who could turn around and get the Billy-ball message across without upsetting rookie players. If that somebody could back up Lou Piniella as hitting coach, as well. . . .

More and more, Willie Horton sounded like the right man for the job. Yet no matter how good the fit, for Willie the decision to leave Detroit wasn't an easy one. It had taken so long to get back to the team and the organization he loved—seven years since the Texas trade—and now he would be going away again. When he called General Manager Bill Lajoie to tell him about it, Willie was almost in tears.

But at last Willie said "yes" to Billy Martin and joined the Yankees—the team traditionally most hated by Detroit—as a "tranquility coach."

Old teammate Al Kaline admitted to reporters that he was surprised that Martin had asked for Willie, at least considering some of the trouble they'd had with each other. But after he thought about it, Kaline realized that Martin must have seen the same thing in Willie that he himself had noticed in spring training that year. Al put it this way:

"[Willie is] mature. . . . [He has] a deep love and affection for the game of baseball. Being around him I saw . . . a good baseball man. He gets along with players. He likes to put the uniform on every day and talk to the players. I was very impressed with how the players looked up to him. They seemed mesmerized by him."

⚾⚾⚾⚾⚾

Whether he could "mesmerize" players or not, Willie's job with the Yankees lasted only as long as Billy Martin's did. Maybe Willie should have been appointed go-between for Martin and Yankee owner George Steinbrenner! By the end of the season, Martin was gone, fired by Steinbrenner yet another time. On this occasion, he was replaced by Lou Piniella. Lou didn't need a "tranquility coach," but by then it didn't matter. Without Billy Martin there, Willie had no interest in staying in New York. He knew where he could go, too. Before the 1985 season ended, "the Hawk," Chicago White Sox General Manager Ken Harrelson, had contacted Steinbrenner asking permission to talk to Willie about coaching for the White Sox.

So the next year brought yet a different job for Willie—this time as the White Sox hitting coach and "coach for player development." Maybe, at last, this would be the "perfect job." At least

THE HORTON FAMILY REUNION. When all the Hortons get together, they make quite a crowd. Here Willie and his wife Gloria (bottom center) sit with two grandchildren between them. (Photo courtesy of Willie Horton.)

it focused on the two things he had learned to do best: hit and work with young people.

As he settled in with Chicago, Willie took a good hard look at his life. Coaching was a delight, but there wasn't any more job stability in coaching than there was on the playing field. Each time he had to change jobs, it hurt. He had to leave friends behind and work unfinished. This bothered Willie more and more. There had to be something he could do, somewhere, that would let him reach out to young people and, at the same time, make a living without going through all these upsetting moves from team to team. His family was still in Seattle. Maybe it was time for everybody to go home to Michigan.

HEADING HOME

There was something wonderfully warm and welcoming about just seeing familiar Detroit landmarks. There was Tiger

Stadium, tucked into the corner of Michigan and Trumbull—big and gray and solid. There were the projects rising high above the Lodge Freeway. Across town, he knew there would be the hustle and bustle of the Eastern Market, where farmers sold fresh produce to city dwellers. Tall office buildings loomed over Detroit's waterfront. Not far from those same buildings, old men sat fishing in the Detroit River. It was Detroit, all right, and it was good to be home.

Unfortunately, being "home" didn't bring with it much improvement in job stability. Instead, Willie's job situation soon felt all too familiar.

Because of some family friendships that dated back to Seattle days, Willie quickly hooked up with Troop, a company that sold athletic apparel. Willie was to run a series of youth programs for Troop—as part of the company's public relations project. This was fine for a while, and then the local Troop franchise owner, rapper M. C. Hammer, shut down his business.

Willie just shook his head in disbelief. He kept doing all that people asked him to do, but the jobs, inside and outside of baseball, just kept evaporating. To have any kind of long-term success, it looked as if he'd have to do something on his own. At least he couldn't fire himself! Maybe, if he worked for himself, he could pick his own goals. He'd find some way, yet, to help kids who needed help. Detroit's legendary priest, Father William (Bill) Cunningham—famous for his "Focus: HOPE" ministries—had some specific ideas to offer.

And so Willie decided to start his own company again. He'd call it Willie Horton City Technologies. The company would train inner-city youth in the use of high-tech equipment—the computers and cable-based home technology that were changing everybody's life. To pay its way, Willie Horton City Technologies would subcontract (work for other companies) in technology-related situations. Once "Technologies" got off the ground, Willie would use the profits to form a "Willie Horton Foundation" to benefit troubled youth. For more direct help to young people who had been in real trouble, he would establish "Horton Houses"—real homes that would function as "safe" houses offering guidance to teens.

Willie knew that "on his own" was a relative term. He didn't want to be dependent on another company that could close down, as the Troop franchise stores had done. But there was no way Willie could do everything he wanted to do without the support of other foundations and of the city itself.

The first person he spoke to about his project was Detroit's long-time mayor, Coleman Young. Mayor Young was a controversial figure. Not only was he the city's first African American mayor, he was a very strong mayor. He ran the city offices his way, and he generally brushed aside anybody who tried to oppose him.

But Young liked Willie. As a matter of fact, for a long time the mayor had been trying to get him to come back to the city, and this was one of the reasons Willie decided to leave the White Sox. Willie liked Coleman Young personally, too. The mayor's attitude toward life reminded Willie a lot of Pop. "If you want to do something to help people, you have to commit yourself [to the project] totally," Mayor Young told Willie, and Willie had to smile. He'd heard that before from Pop, almost word for word.

Supported by Mayor Young and other prominent Detroiters, Willie Horton City Technologies became a reality—but that was all. Sadly, it didn't look as if the company ever would earn very much money—at least not enough money for the foundation and Horton Houses to happen. Willie was sure he had the right idea, and he was proud of what he'd accomplished, but so far, he still hadn't found the way to go about it.

P.A.L.

After Detroit's terrible riots in 1967, the city government looked for ways to reach out to children living in the poorer neighborhoods. There had to be a way to keep young people, particularly minority young people, from thinking that all authority was bad and that the police were "pigs."

In March 1969, under Mayor Roman Gribbs, the city decided that the best "reach-out" would come from the police themselves. That spring, the Detroit Police Athletic League (P.A.L.) was formed. Through P.A.L., police officers would help Detroit young people participate in all kinds of organized sports—from baseball to skiing, golf to football.

P.A.L. was an actual unit of the police department, authorized by the mayor and supported by the chief of police. It quickly became a prominent part of life in Detroit. Endorsed by the most important people in town, it reached out to thousands of youngsters through thousands of programs.

In 1989, Mayor Young came to Willie with a proposal. Would Willie be interested in being deputy director of the twenty-year-old Police Athletic League? Never had Willie said "yes" to a job offer so quickly!

He was tickled to death. He'd be working with people like National Football League (N.F.L.) Hall of Famer Dick "Night Train" Lane—and Detroit's radio giant J. P. McCarthy. It was a dream job. He couldn't imagine anything more perfect. He threw himself into it the way he would have suited up for a critical ball game. The mayor was just as pleased. He'd been impressed by Willie's commitment to young people during the time that Willie Horton City Technologies was being established. It would be fun to see what Willie could do with an organization like P.A.L. at his disposal.

Willie was an outstanding P.A.L. director. But the more things changed, the more they stayed the same.

In four years, Dennis Archer replaced Coleman Young as mayor. Like new managers everywhere, he brought in his own people to operate a great many of the city programs. All over town, people who had been appointed by Coleman Young suddenly found that they no longer had jobs. The Police Athletic League didn't escape. Once again, Willie was out of a job.

Willie understood why Mayor Archer preferred to work with his own people, but he couldn't help wondering whether Archer was doing the right thing. When Willie joined P.A.L., there had been 10,000 active P.A.L. programs. When he left, there were 25,000. His would be a very hard act to follow.

TURNING FANTASY INTO REALITY

More than twenty years after the Tigers met the Cardinals in the World Series, the City of Detroit still loved the 1968 club as they'd loved no other Tiger team. Even the 1984 World Champions didn't belong to the people quite the way that Willie and the other boys from Syracuse had done.

When people love something that much, somebody will usually find a way to sell it to them and make money. Capitalizing on the way that people felt about the '68 Tigers, a local Detroit businessman, Jerry Lewis, teamed up with Willie's old teammate Jim Price to begin a series of "fantasy camps." Going to one of these camps was just like attending regular baseball spring training sessions—only anybody could go. Campers weren't ballplayers at all. They were just ordinary men who loved baseball. A few of them could really play—maybe had played in high school or college—but a lot of campers had never done more than play softball with their friends. Now they'd be out on the same diamond with people like Al Kaline and Mickey Stanley—and Willie Horton!

Everything was done to make the people who enrolled feel as if they were in a real spring training camp. Campers were issued uniforms, and baseball cards were printed with their pictures on them. Every day they got to play ball with their heroes, and every night they had dinner and sat there and swapped baseball stories with major league ballplayers. So that "real" major league fields could be used, the camps took place before spring training began.

The men who came to play and train in the fantasy camps arrived in all ages, shapes, and sizes. Some played ball regularly. Some hadn't walked out onto a playing field since they were children. Some of them were sixty or seventy years old. Some were even older, and yet others were just out of college. Most of the campers were an age that fell somewhere in between. There were businessmen and teachers and doctors and college students. The single thing they had in common was a love for baseball and a love for the Tigers.

Fantasy camps were a great experience for everyone, and one that Willie was glad to support. It wasn't exactly like coaching youth from the streets of Detroit, but Willie thoroughly enjoyed teaching campers to improve their baseball skills. He enjoyed meeting the people, too—although, once camp was over, he didn't expect to see them again unless they came back the next year.

Playing in a fantasy camp wasn't cheap. Most of the men who attended were successful businessmen—people who could afford to spend two or three thousand dollars each for a week's vacation. One of these was Bob Milano, president and part owner of O.R.T. Tool Company. Milano was young, energetic, a "good guy," and a lot of fun to have in camp—but Willie was hardly prepared for the day the "good guy" came up to him and asked to talk seriously for a minute.

In a rush, Milano explained that Willie had meant a lot to him throughout his life—and not just for the things that happened on the playing field or in camp. Milano was impressed by Willie's pride, integrity, and ability to dream and work hard. Willie, he said earnestly, was exactly the person O.R.T. Tool needed on its national accounts sales team.

People selling to national accounts earn good money. Willie thought about it . . . though not too seriously, at least not at first. Gates Brown and the other former Tigers in camp just laughed.

But Milano was very serious. Before Willie even made it back to Detroit after the camp closed for the year, Milano telephoned Gloria to tell her of the opportunity he had for her husband. That phone call was a good move on Milano's part. It probably did as much as anything else he could have done to convince Willie the job offer was "for real."

Willie headed back to Detroit, never dreaming that he was about to go to work for O.R.T. Tool. He'd certainly not been trying to sell himself to anybody. He'd just liked the man. Yet the more he thought about it, the more he liked the whole idea. When he got home, he talked to Gloria—and he took the job. He would work with both Detroit and national accounts.

Willie found one new project in fantasy camp. He found the next one in the dentist's office!

While he was waiting in his dentist's lobby, Willie fell into conversation with an executive from Ford Motor Company. It was hard for Willie to talk about Detroit *without* talking about the things he wanted to be able to do for its young people, and the Ford executive proved to be a very willing audience. Soon, Willie was headed home bubbling with a new idea.

Willie Horton Industries, Inc., was begun as a partnership involving Willie, all three of Detroit's "big three" automotive companies (Ford, General Motors, and Chrysler), and Caterpillar Tractor. The main purpose of the company was to create jobs for young men and women. After a time, other established business-men, including some of the executives at O.R.T. Tool, joined Willie Horton Industries as mentors for the job seekers.

Fulfilling their part of the arrangement, the big manufactur-ers would help Willie train inner-city youth in the skills needed to be successful in the machine tool, automotive, or electronics business. Willie wished Father Bill Cunningham were still alive to see it. It was exactly the sort of thing the priest had sketched out in those months when Willie first came back to Detroit from the White Sox.

And, in the meantime, Willie still could help O.R.T. Tool with its national accounts.

All because of a chance meeting in the dentist's office!

⚾⚾⚾ 13 ⚾⚾⚾
The Biggest Thrill of All

THANK YOU, WILLIE HORTON

"As long as I'm around baseball, I'm happy," Willie told the reporter. The year was 1985, but it could have been almost any year in Willie's life. "My teammates were always my family, my ballpark was my home, and baseball was my life. I can't ever give back to baseball the love and respect the game has given me. . . .

"I like the ballparks, I like the people, I like the atmosphere. I like the smell of fresh uniforms hanging up in the clubhouse. I just like being around, being involved. . . . I'd like to stay in the game until I pass away."

Whether he was working for O.R.T. Tool, for Willie Horton Industries, or as an instructor in a fantasy camp, there was little doubt that Willie was still "in the game." Baseball was part of him, and he of it.

But there was another part of Willie that was just as important as baseball. As a matter of fact, it usually was very hard to tell where baseball left off and Willie's other dream began. That dream, of course, was helping "the kids," helping young people of all races, all backgrounds, in the hope and belief that, through them, the world could be made into a better place. After all, Willie believed that anything he ever accomplished happened because an opportunity was given to him by somebody else—and, to Willie, that meant he had an obligation to give it all back in some way.

Over the years, awards began to pile up as people discovered how very much Willie was giving back to his community. He earned the Spirit of Detroit Award. He was asked to represent baseball as a worldwide Ambassador of Goodwill. He was honored by the Knights of Columbus and by the New Light Baptist Church. J. C. Penney Corporation honored him, as did the Michigan Heart Association. He was named "Father of the Year" and "Unsung Hero of Sport." He was inducted into the Michigan Sports Hall of Fame in 1987, the International Afro-American Hall of Fame in 1992, and the Military Hall of Fame in 1998 (the latter for the many, many trips he made to speak at military installations worldwide). The Syracuse Chiefs added him to their "Wall" of Fame in 2000. The awards continued to pour in, and, all the while, Willie kept giving back more and more. He did volunteer work for the United Way and for the Boys and Girls Clubs of America. He provided Meals on Wheels and worked with the Foundation Fighting Blindness.

And he still walked through his old neighborhood in Detroit, talking, talking, talking to young people he met in the street—in the hope that he could turn them in the right direction.

In late September 1999, Willie put on the uniform he loved and walked out in front of the fans at Tiger Stadium for the last time. The occasion was the final Tiger game ever to be played at the corner of Michigan and Trumbull. After one hundred years, the team was moving across town to play in a new, modern facility.

After the last out, the last pitch ever made on that playing field, the crowd was quiet. They'd been told something wonderful would happen, but no one knew what it would be. The field was empty; the fans waited. Then the big gates to the old bullpen in center opened, and history walked out onto the playing field.

Led in seniority by eighty-nine-year-old Eldon Auker, who'd last pitched for the Tigers in 1938, former Tiger after former Tiger trotted out onto the field and took his position. There were no formal announcements of names—just the swelling voices of fans passing the word as they spotted each familiar face. Most people in the old park felt as if they were watching their entire lives pass before them.

Willie almost said he wouldn't be part of it. He didn't want to say goodbye to a place that had meant so much to him. He wasn't even sure that he could bear it. "I said a prayer and asked God to get me through it," he said.

When it was his turn to run out toward left field, he waved his cap to the fans. The roar of recognition was deafening. "Willie!" "Willie!" people shouted—first to each other, and then to Willie himself. "Willie Horton!" "It's Willie the Wonder!"

THE LAST GAME. No matter where else he played baseball, Tiger Stadium was Willie's home. Sadly, after the 1999 season, that home would be no more. Giving way to the demand for a more modern ballpark, the Tigers played their last game at the Corner on September 27, 1999. That night, fans flocked across the streets and poured past the turnstiles to say farewell to the oldest ballpark then in use in the major leagues. (Photo by K. E. Bush.)

Willie ducked his head. His eyes were so full of tears he could hardly see. He loved the fans, the place, the game so much he felt as if he couldn't stand it. Somehow he made his way to left field. Larry Herndon, who'd played on the 1984 World Championship team, was there to welcome him. Herndon threw his arms around Willie. "Let it out, brother," Herndon said. "This is your home."

FOREVER A TIGER

"I've had plenty of thrills in baseball, but the biggest one is just putting on this uniform." Willie spoke to a reporter as he dressed for a game back in 1975. "I'm proud to be a Tiger," he

THANK YOU, WILLIE HORTON. On the day the Tigers retired Willie's number 23, Willie spoke to the crowd at Comerica Park. He tried to tell them how he would always be a Tiger and how much the honor of having his number retired meant to him. He choked back tears as he spoke. So much of his life was summed up in what happened that day. (Photo by Mike Litaker.)

went on. "I hope to keep putting on No. 23 and to be a credit to it. I want the kids to look up to me. Somebody else will be wearing this uniform some day, and when I see that I want to feel that I was a good example all the years I had it."

In the summer of 2000, the Detroit Tigers saw to it that the example Willie set for young people while wearing that uniform was something that would never be forgotten.

It's not very often that a ballplayer's number is "retired." Retiring a number means that no one else may ever wear that number for the team again—ever. In the one hundred years the Tigers had been in existence, they had retired the numbers of only four players: Charlie Gehringer (2), Hank Greenberg (5), Al Kaline (6), and Hal Newhouser (16). They would have retired Ty Cobb's number, but in the days when Cobb played, there weren't any numbers on the uniforms.

FRIENDS. Something as important as retiring a number and unveiling a statue requires an appropriate audience. When the Tigers retired number 23, as many as possible of the 1968 Tigers assembled in the Comerica outfield. Here fellow '68 teammate Earl Wilson gives Willie a hug, as Mickey Stanley (arrow), one of the boys from Syracuse, looks on. (Photo by Mike Litaker.)

Now they were going to retire number 23. No one but Willie could ever use it again—not even World Series hero Kirk Gibson, who'd worn it during the 1984 season.

Willie could hardly believe it, but retiring his number was only a small part of the honor that was going to be paid him.

The new Comerica Park, the modern structure that replaced Tiger Stadium, featured its own Hall of Fame. Above and beyond the left field wall, ballpark designers had placed larger than life statues of five of the greatest Tigers ever to play in old Tiger Stadium. Each one was shown doing what he did best. Frozen forever in time, Ty Cobb slid into base, spikes high. Charlie Gehringer pivoted at second base, ready to double off the runner. Hank Greenberg took his mighty home run swing. Hal

THE BIGGEST THRILL OF ALL

THE WILLIE HORTON STATUE, COMERICA PARK. The inscription on the plaque below the statue reads:

WILLIE HORTON
"Willie the Wonder"

Born: October 18, 1942 (Arno, Virginia)

Detroit Tigers (OF, DH) 1963–77

Texas Rangers, Cleveland Indians, Toronto Blue Jays (DH, OF) 1978

Seattle Mariners (DH) 1979–1980

A hometown hero whose accomplishments on and off the field are a credit to the city of Detroit.

ACHIEVEMENTS AND HONORS

Raised in a Detroit housing project and overcame adversity to become a Tiger hometown hero

Was a baseball star for Detroit's Northwestern High School and played Detroit sandlot baseball

Was instrumental in helping crush the violence that erupted during the 1967 riots in Detroit

Batted .326 his first season with the Tigers

Had 100 or more RBI in 1965 (104) and 1966 (100)

Threw out Lou Brock at home plate in the pivotal game five of the 1968 World Series

Led the team in home runs 1968 (36), 1969 (28) and 1975 (25)

Hit 325 career home runs, 1,163 RBI, and had a .273 lifetime batting average

Was elected to four All Star teams as a Tiger

Had his uniform number 23 retired July 15, 2000

Sculptors: Julie & Omri R. Amrany. Co-sculptor: Gary Tillery
Dedicated: July 15, 2000

(Photo by K. E. Bush.)

CHAPTER 13

Newhouser, caught in the middle of a full windup, kicked his leg high. Al Kaline stretched for a fly ball that any other outfielder would have let go over his head.

⚾⚾⚾⚾⚾

Thirty-nine years before, just as Willie was ready to sign his rookie contract with the Detroit Tigers, Pop had reached out and grabbed his wrist—hard. "If you can't make a total commitment now that your life belongs to the fans, don't sign that contract," Pop told him.

For most of the following thirty-nine years just being in baseball—whether playing, coaching, or participating in the fantasy camps—was the greatest joy Willie could imagine. Keeping his commitment to the fans was easy. Yes, there had been times when things didn't go right. But the same faith that kept Willie walking down the railroad track from Stonega, Virginia, to Appalachia still kept telling him that baseball was where he belonged—that baseball was where he could do the most for other people.

Over and over again, baseball had done things for Willie, too. He thought of all the times he'd said to himself, "Man, oh, man, I've never been so happy in my life." When the Tigers won the Series; when he made those eleven putouts; when he hit his 300th home run; when Seattle gave the "ancient Mariner" his own day. . . .

But he'd never been this happy. This was truly the biggest thrill of all.

Of course they'd told him what they were going to do. Of course he knew it was going to be there. But he still couldn't believe it.

Willie stood there staring at the silvery-gray metal statues above the Comerica Park outfield. Now the empty spot to their left was empty no more. The Detroit Tigers had placed a sixth statue there. This one showed a husky batter, a fellow with bulging muscles, lunging forward as he followed through on his swing. The sculptors had worked and worked to make it so that anybody looking at the statue could feel the sheer force of that swing. People had to be able to tell that this was a player who swung a bat so hard that, if the swing were checked, the end of the bat would snap right off.

Willie Horton, proudly wearing Tiger uniform number 23, would be in uniform at Comerica Park forever.

146

AFTERWORD

Willie's story goes on and on. The statue at Comerica stands there to remind generations that a very special sort of ballplayer once wore uniform number 23 for the Tigers. From the outside, new honors come from all directions. For Detroit's year-long three-hundredth birthday celebration (throughout 2001), Dearborn's famed Greenfield Village and Edison Institute wanted to create a special tricentennial film for their spectacular IMAX theater. To chronicle the history of Detroit correctly, sports had to be included. Seeking the single best living representative of baseball in Detroit for all the years that baseball had been played there, the institute came to Willie Horton.

Then, just as work was concluded on the text for this book, Willie became a Detroit Tiger again—at least in a way! In 2001, the Tigers were no longer anything like the team they had been in 1968. The players struggled on the field, and many seats in shiny new Comerica Park stayed empty, game after game. People criticized the way the whole organization was run. The Tigers needed help, and to whom did they turn? To Willie and his 1968 teammate Al Kaline. Kaline was asked to do what he could to help rebuild the baseball team. Willie, determined to bring back the "Tiger mystique," would keep on doing everything else he was doing—with young people, with O.R.T. Tool, with the Willie Horton Foundation. But now he also would step back into his role as Designated Healer, helping to bring the team he loves and the town he loves closer together.

And while all *this* is going on, Willie continues to create his own memorials—more significant than any outside honor handed him. Stories keep emerging: about the time that he saw a house burning on Trumbull Avenue near Tiger Stadium and took in the whole family, later buying them a new house—or

147

how Jim Campbell thought so much of Willie that he left him quite a lot of money in his will.

At the time this book went to press, the Willie Horton Foundation was reaching out to the children in the Tri-City region of Virginia and Tennessee,* seeking to help those who were growing up—all too often in poverty—in the same world Willie knew as a boy. Through Willie's two-year-old "Grand Slam" charity, young people advance around four important bases.

First base makes it possible for the children to fit into their immediate environment. By partnering with another foundation, Grand Slam provides new clothes and new school supplies for young people who otherwise would have nothing. The key word is "new." Willie remembers well the feeling of self-respect that came along with the new clothes that people like Ron Thompson and Sam Bishop gave him.

Second base brings Tri-City children face-to-face with mentors who will train them in the technology necessary for success in today's business world. Third base emphasizes their preparation for college and includes both tutorial programs and scholarship funding.

As they pass each "base," each stage in their lives, the children are taught to volunteer for things—to start to give something back to their community. All his life Willie has felt that he needs to "give back" to society—to make up for what he owes those who helped him while he was growing up. Now, young people in the Grand Slam program learn that the process of being given an advantage doesn't stop with the advantage. If they have been given a break, they also have been handed the responsibility to do something for others.

Once a child has circled all the bases and reached "home plate," Willie—and the dedicated people administering the program—believe that child will be prepared for a successful life.

To help raise money for Grand Slam, Willie has begun a series of fund-raising "Baseball Weekends for Children." Professional athletes are brought in to Kingsport, Tennessee, to speak to young people in a baseball setting. When Monica Patrick—Willie's grand-niece who administers the program—

---

* The "Tri-Cities" are Kingsport, Tennessee; Johnson City, Tennessee; and Bristol, Tennessee/Virginia.

first began calling possible contributors, she was amazed. Over and over, when she spoke to the men with whom Willie had played, she heard the same thing. "If Willie wants us there, we'll be there. When do you need us?"

In gratitude for Willie's concern for the state's youth, the governor of Virginia chose May of 2001 to induct Willie into the Virginia State Hall of Fame. In 2002, it will be the governor of Tennessee's turn to extend Willie the same honor from his state.

As the Grand Slam/Tri-City program grows and matures, it is becoming a prototype for similar efforts nationwide. Recently, the state of Kentucky approached Willie and asked for information on the program. Many people in Detroit are looking forward to the day that Willie is able to bring Grand Slam to Michigan.

And, meanwhile, back home in Detroit, Willie and the Willie Horton Foundation are working on yet another project—this time one that seeks to reopen and reequip the New Haven (Michigan) school district's trade academy. The academy will provide both young people and adults in Macomb and St. Clair counties with training in a variety of technical skills. Questioned by a reporter about the thought behind the effort to reopen the school, Willie's son Al Horton had a ready answer. "This is a love affair for my father," he said. "[His dedication to the area and to young people] will last forever."

As for Willie, he figures he's just continuing on down the road that God set him on the day that He started him down the railroad tracks toward Appalachia.

Talkin' Baseball (A Glossary)

Most of us know the ordinary terms in baseball—things like "ball" and "strike" and "home plate"—so those aren't included here. Instead, this list is intended to help you with some of the strange combinations of words that players and fans use when they start "talkin' baseball." Most of the following expressions are used somewhere in this book.

according to the book: Certain things in baseball can be predicted. For example, right-handed batters usually find it easier to hit pitches thrown by left-handed pitchers. Whenever a manager or a player does something just because the law of averages says it will work out better that way, he is said to be doing whatever it is "according to the book."

batting average: A baseball player's batting average is determined by dividing the number of hits he has by the number of times he has come to bat. The result is shown as a three-digit decimal number, but it's read as if the decimal point weren't there. For example: If a man comes to bat a hundred times and gets thirty hits, he is batting .300. Mathematicians would read that number "three hundred thousandths." In baseball, people just say the man is "batting three hundred." A batting average over .350 is outstanding; .300 is very good; .275 is respectable. Anything below .250 isn't very good at all, and below .200 is a disaster.

batting cleanup: The person who bats fourth in the lineup (the list of the order in which people come to bat) is said to be bat-

151

ting cleanup. If any of the first three batters gets on base, the cleanup hitter is in a position to drive in the runner(s)—that is, "clean up" the bases with a home run or base hit.

bearing down: When a player bears down, he is concentrating and doing his best.

between the foul lines: This literally means "on the playing field." The expression usually refers to the time a ballplayer spends actually playing baseball. Of a good player with a lousy personality, you might say that "He is a good guy to have between the foul lines, but off the field he's a real jerk."

"Billy-ball": Billy Martin was a very aggressive ballplayer. He'd do almost anything to win. When he managed, he expected his players to play the same way. His fighting, running, hustling style of baseball became known as "Billy-ball."

cheap hit: A ball that isn't hit very hard, but still is neither a foul nor an out, is a "cheap hit." A cheap hit can "go through" the infielders either because a fielder is playing in the wrong position or just because the batter is lucky.

checked swing: A checked swing occurs when a batter starts his swing but decides, for whatever reason, to stop it. A swing isn't "checked" unless the bat is stopped before it crosses the plate. Sometimes a batter will check his swing and hit the ball anyway, by accident. If he does that, the ball is in play, just as if he were swinging away.

clubhouse: The players' dressing room, lockers, and shower area make up the clubhouse. In a major league ballpark, a clubhouse also includes weight rooms, trainers' rooms, and all kinds of other things that players use to get ready for the game.

come from behind: When a team is behind in the score during the first part of a game and then scores enough runs to win, they have won a "come from behind" victory.

"the Corner": Tiger Stadium sits at the corner of Michigan and Trumbull Avenues. Over the years, Tiger fans began to talk about seeing baseball "at the Corner" without bothering to name the streets or the stadium.

cutoff man: The infielder who is positioned to take a throw from the outfield and either hold it or relay it to complete a play is called the "cutoff man."

designated hitter ("D.H."): In 1973, the American League adopted a rule that allowed managers to name a single pinch hitter to bat for the pitcher during an entire game. Before the designated hitter rule came into effect, each time a man batted for a pitcher, he replaced the pitcher, and a new pitcher had to be brought into the game. Similarly, unless the pinch hitter stayed in the game to play a position, he was done once he finished batting. The next time the manager needed a pinch hitter, he had to use somebody else.

With the designated hitter rule, older players can stay in major league ball as D.H.'s, even after they are no longer fast enough or healthy enough to play a regular position. However, a lot of people don't like the designated hitter rule because it limits the pitcher to being just a defensive player and, in effect, "takes him out of the game." Having a D.H. also reduces the number of decisions a manager has to make. Many people believe having a designated hitter makes the game boring.

double play: This is sometimes called "two for the price of one." A double play happens when the ball is hit (or is in play) only once but two men are called out. This can occur in a number of different ways, but very often it happens when a player already on first base runs to second when the ball is hit. He is tagged or thrown out, and then the ball is thrown back to first in time for the batter to be put out as well. The play at second is termed a "force-out" because the runner has to run to second. He has no choice. He must make room for the batter running toward first.

down three to one: "Down three to one," or "down five to two," or "down" any such number, refers to the score from the point of view of the team that is getting the worst of things. If you are down three to one in a game, you are behind by two runs—trailing three to one. If you are down three to one in a series, you have lost three games and have won only one time.

drill him: "Drilling" somebody is an expression meaning the pitcher has hit the batter with a pitch, usually with a fast ball (a ball thrown very hard).

dropped two straight games: Dropping a game means losing a game—in this case, two in a row. Sometimes this phrase is used to mean a game was lost carelessly or unnecessarily, but usually it just means that a team didn't win.

E.R.A.: E.R.A. stands for "earned run average." This number reflects how many runs a pitcher would allow to score if he pitched all nine innings. It is calculated by adding up the number of runs scored against a pitcher and then adding up the number of innings he has pitched. The number of runs scored is divided by the actual number of innings pitched to find out how many runs a pitcher allows each inning, and then that number is multiplied by nine. Most good pitchers have earned run averages of about 3.50 or 3.60. E.R.A.s below 3.00 are excellent, and E.R.A.s below 2.00 are rare and very, very special.

field a team/field a player: This has nothing to do with fielding or catching a ball. If a town "fields a team," it just means that it has one. A team that "fields some good players" has some good players on its team.

full windup: If a pitcher goes through his entire motion—the moves that he makes before he lets go of the ball—he is said to be taking a full windup. This usually involves holding the ball in one hand, hiding that hand with the baseball glove worn on the other hand, pumping both hands up and down, and then rocking backward on one foot to get momentum for the throw. Some players rock backward so far they kick one leg high in the air. Early in the twentieth century, a lot of pitchers actually spun their arms around and around like windmills before they let go of the ball!

gathering splinters: Baseball slang for not playing in a game but, instead, sitting on the bench in the dugout. Benches used to be made of wood, hence the term "gathering splinters."

get a better jump on the ball: "Getting a jump on the ball" occurs when an outfielder starts running "with the crack of the bat"—heading in the direction a batted ball will take before it has reached the outfield. The term "getting a jump on" also is used to describe a runner who is trying to steal a base. If the runner can get far enough toward the base he is trying to steal, he is said to have "gotten a good jump on" the pitcher (or the catcher, depending on when he gets his jump).

getting around on the ball (or getting all the way around on the ball): If a batter swings the bat rapidly enough that it meets the ball squarely and the batted ball stays in fair territory, he has "got around" on the ball. A player who is not getting around on the ball will hit a lot of foul balls to the opposite field (see below). Home run hitters who swing late and don't get around on the ball sometimes find that a ball that could have gone far enough to be out of the park becomes just another opposite field or center field putout.

giving 200 percent: A player who tries as hard as he can very single minute of the time is doing more than the usual 100 percent effort, so he's "giving 200 percent."

go all the way: In Willie's playing days, this meant being ahead during the season, winning a league championship, and going on to win the World Series. Nowadays, to "go all the way" teams need first to win a divisional playoff, then the league championship, and then the series.

grand slam: A home run hit with the "bases loaded"—that is, with runners on all three bases—is a grand slam home run. With one stroke of the bat, four runs score.

grapefruit season: Spring training camps in Florida are in the "Grapefruit League," and so the games they play are part of "grapefruit season." When Willie first signed with the Tigers, just about all spring training camps were in Florida. Now there is also a spring training "Cactus League," named for the teams that work out in Arizona.

hitting behind the runner: If a batted ball is hit on the ground so that it bounces through the infield, it's better for a base runner if it goes to the right side—behind the runner as he hurries around the bases. That way the runner isn't running toward the player who has the ball in his hand, and who can tag him out. Some batters can control where they will hit the ball well enough so they can hit behind a runner on purpose, in order to give him the best chance to score. (Also see "opposite field hit.")

hit (or hitting) for average: This is a quick way to say that a batter is more concerned about a high batting average than he is about hitting home runs. Sometimes it's appropriate to say that a player "hits the long ball, but can hit for average, too."

late innings: "Late innings" usually refers to the seventh, eighth, and ninth innings of a ball game.

the long ball: "Long ball" means a home run. A batter who "hits the long ball" hits a lot of home runs.

loss/lost column: When newspapers print baseball standings (who is ahead of whom in the league), they do it in a series of columns. One column contains team names. Another shows how many games each team has won, and yet another, the "loss" (sometimes "lost") column, shows how many games each team has lost. Once a team has lost a game, there's no way to get it back again. It's very important to have as few games as possible in the loss column, even when a team is leading the league.

off-season: The off-season is the part of the year between the World Series and spring training, when major league baseball is not being played—that is, from October through early February.

on the fly: A batted ball that is caught before it hits the ground has been caught "on the fly."

opposite field hit: If a right-handed batter gets all the way around on the ball (see above) he usually will hit it to the left. A left-handed batter usually will hit to the right. If, instead, the right-hander hits to right field, he's said to have hit to the "opposite field" from where the ball normally would go. Hitting to the opposite field can take more strength than hitting the ball hard in the "right" direction. However, hitting to the opposite field on purpose is an important skill. For example, a ball hit to the opposite field by a right-handed batter lands "behind the runner," making it easier for a runner to score.

parent club: A major league ball club that has an organization of minor league teams is the "parent" of each minor league club.

pennant/win the pennant: Winning the pennant means the same as winning the league championship. There is a National League pennant and an American League pennant. The World Series is a play-off between the teams that have won the National and American League pennants for that year.

platooned: When a manager makes a point of playing right-handed hitters against left-handed pitchers, or vice versa, he is platooning his players.

pressing: A player is pressing when he tries so hard that the pressure he puts on himself keeps him from doing as well as he really can.

R.B.I.: R.B.I. is the abbreviation for "runs batted in." Even though the "R" stands for "runs," baseball people talk about "R.B.I.'s" (or "ribbies") in the plural. Runs that score when a batter gets a hit usually count as part of his total R.B.I.'s. (There are several rules that can affect whether or not this is the case.) A player who has 100 R.B.I.'s in a year has done an outstanding job.

right down the middle: If a pitch crosses the middle of home plate, and it is very easy to tell that the pitch is in the strike zone, it is said to have been thrown "right down the middle."

rookie: The first year a player is in the major leagues, he is called a "rookie," even if he has spent years and years in the minor leagues. His rookie year in the majors is the first year that really counts.

running on the pitch: A base runner is running on the pitch if he starts running toward the next base before the batter begins to swing at the ball. He does this to give himself a better chance of reaching second (or third, or home) without being thrown out.

scoring position: A base runner on second or third base is in "scoring position" because he is likely to have time to run all the way to home plate if the batter hits the ball out of the infield.

set position: If there are runners on base, pitchers don't usually take a full windup. Instead, they "set" themselves on the pitcher's mound, rock backward, then throw the ball. (See "full windup.")

shag flies: During batting practice, a great many baseballs are hit into the outfield. Players who stay in the outfield to catch these balls and toss them back into the infield to be used again are "shagging" fly balls.

starter: The word "starter," as most frequently used, refers to a starting pitcher. Teams field "starters" and "relievers." Starters begin the game; relievers come into the game whenever a starting pitcher is removed.

starting assignment: "Starting assignment" is a little more general than just "starter." A man has a "starting assignment" in left field (or any other position) if he starts the game playing there. If a player has "earned a starting assignment" in a position," he probably is pretty good. Remember, though—if the specific position isn't named (as in "starting the game in right field"), "starting for the home team" almost always refers to a pitcher.

statistics: Baseball uses so many numbers to keep track of how well players and teams are doing, that the numbers, or "stats" (short for "statistics") become an essential part of the game for people who follow it closely. Some fans spend the entire off-season talking about the stats.

sweet spot: The place on the barrel of the bat where it is the strongest and the most resilient (springy). A ball hit "on the sweet spot" usually will go straighter and carry farther than one hit either "on the handle" or on the end of the bat.

tearing up the league: When a batter is hitting the ball so well that he is driving in a lot of runs and scoring a lot himself, he is said to be "tearing up the league" offensively.

veteran: A ballplayer who is several years beyond his rookie year is a veteran. How soon he begins to be considered a veteran sometimes depends on how many younger players there are on his team!

winter ball: The regular season for baseball in South America and the Caribbean (for example, Puerto Rico, the Dominican Republic, Venezuela) extends into the North American winter. Therefore, a player who plays on a Venezuelan team in January is playing "winter ball," even though it's really summer in Venezuela.

ACKNOWLEDGMENTS

So many "acknowledgments" pages begin with the words, "this book would not have been possible without. . . ." In the case of *Willie Horton*, the statement is literally true.

Any research into the life of a sports figure must be heavily dependent on newspaper coverage of his achievements. Willie's book is no exception. While preparing his initial draft, Grant Eldridge drew on half-a-dozen feature articles that appeared in the *Detroit News* or *Detroit Free Press*. These provided a basic framework for Willie's story. For day-to-day details of Willie's life off and on the field, Karen Bush turned to the National Baseball Hall of Fame. The Hall maintains an extensive library, and they were extremely generous in providing access to their entire collection of "Willie" information. While the author is fortunate in that she has four lengthy scrapbooks of her own that cover the Tigers during Willie's first years with the team, she is heavily indebted to the Hall for its ability to provide exclusive focus on Willie's achievements and documentation of his activities after he left Detroit.

Staffs of the Walter P. Reuther Library (Wayne State University) and the Burton Historical Collection (Detroit Public Library)—especially Tom Featherstone and David Poremba—were particularly helpful in researching photographic documentation of Willie's life and times, as were representatives of the *Detroit News* photo library. Individual photographers, acknowledged separately in various photo credits, were equally enthusiastic about their contribution to the overall project.

Special thanks go to Roy Rogers, Jr., who recalled his dad's love for the game and eagerly presented author Karen Bush with an entire sheaf of photographs of his famous father—with the comment that for baseball, for Willie's book, she could have her choice of them.

We owe another special "thank you" to Dr. Larry Latimore, principal of Northwestern High School, for his cooperation. It took some effort for him to locate, and then provide, copies of the school yearbooks that depict Willie's high school baseball career.

Books consulted in the course of research include, among others: Hal Butler's *The Willie Horton Story* (New York: Julian Messner, 1970), George Cantor's *The Tigers of '68, Baseball's Last Real Champions* (Dallas: Taylor Publishing, 1997), Richard Bak and Charlie Vincent's *The Corner: A Century of Memories at Michigan and Trumbull* (Chicago: Triumph, 1999)—and no fewer than seventeen issues of *The Detroit Tigers Official Yearbook* (Detroit Baseball Company, Detroit: privately published, 1961–1977). Miscellaneous television news and interview footage in Karen Bush's private collection proved invaluable, as did Joe Falls and Irwin Cohen's wonderful anthology of oral history, *Echoes of Tiger Stadium* (Southfield, Michigan: Primeau Productions, 1999).

The Internet is a gold mine of statistical and biographical information about Willie Horton. Willie's employer, O.R.T. Tools, maintains online information about their star representative, but ultimately it was the combined force of *Sports Illustrated* magazine and CNN whose definitive statistical reference (http://sportsillustrated.cnn.com/baseball/mlb/all-time_stats/) did most to guarantee the accuracy of specific numbers quoted in *Willie Horton*.

Above all, this book owes its existence to Willie Horton himself, who patiently answered the probably redundant interview questions of two authors—and who repeatedly assured us both that, if this book was going to be for "the kids," or would help "the kids" in any way, he—Willie—would do what he could to guarantee its success.